All the
Words
We
Know

Also by Bruce Nash

An Island in the Lake
The Long River of Cat Fisher

All the Words We Know

A Novel

BRUCE NASH

ATRIA BOOKS

New York   Amsterdam/Antwerp   London
Toronto   Sydney/Melbourne   New Delhi

ATRIA BOOKS

An Imprint of Simon & Schuster, LLC
1230 Avenue of the Americas
New York, NY 10020

For Ollie Nash and Muriel "Joy" Milliken

All the
Words
We
Know

In the beginning is the whatsitsname. The woman in the parking lot. She wears a nightgown and lies on her back, looking up at the sky. The nightgown is white and embroidered at the neck with blue . . . what do you call them? Forget-me-nots. A small crowd is gathered around her. All in their unicorns. Uniforms. All younger than the woman, much younger. They look at each other. They look up at the sky. They look down at the woman. They whisper.

I see them as I come out of the thing—the elevator. I push my walker across the foyer to the big sliding entrance doors and look at them through the glass. From here I can see the woman's neckline with its blue forget-me-nots. There is nothing wrong with my eyesight.

I can see that they are whispering through the glass. I can see, through the glass, that they are whispering. In this place, they always whisper. Or else they shout, so you'll understand them. There is the Doctor, or whatever he is, the Angry Nurse, the Filipino girl and several others, as well as the nice boy who mops the floors. And the woman in the nightgown. She isn't whispering. She is intent on the sky. Intent upon the sky. Upon. Not a word you hear much. The woman is my age, and her nightgown is much like my own, except for the whatsitsnames around the neck. And I wouldn't be wearing a nightgown in the parking lot. I get dressed whenever I leave my room. A proper dress or pantsuit, a decent blouse. I make the effort.

They look at her as if she is a delivery that has arrived unexpectedly. Will they accept the delivery? Every day there are deliveries. Every day trucks arrive in the parking lot and through the big sliding entrance doors come fellows wheeling upright trolley things stacked with boxes. And once, if I recall correctly, a famous cannibal, although that seems unlikely. But whether they are boxes or Hannibals, they always come with papers that need signing by the Angry Nurse. Is that what they're waiting for? The paperwork? Is the woman in the nightgown a delivery that has arrived without paperwork?

No. She must be a new president. Resident. Of course. They're just waiting for an available bed. Usually, the new ones arrive in wheelchairs. Usually, they don't lie out there on their backs in the parking lot, looking at the sky. I imagine that she won't be there for long nevertheless. When there's a bed available in this place, it's never for long. Never the less.

I go back up in the revelator, elevator, to my own floor. I push my walker along the corridor. My son has tied a piece of silk to the door handle of my room. Or my daughter. So that I know it is my room. My son. My daughter. My room.

But before I get to my own room, I go to my friend's room. I know her door because it doesn't have a piece of silk tied to it. Her door is open, so I look inside, but my friend isn't there. What is strange is that her wheelchair is there, and my friend isn't. It stands there, sits there, by the window that looks out over the parking lot. My friend doesn't go anywhere except in that wheelchair.

I am the mobile one. I have my walker and go anywhere I want to in this place, whether I'm supposed to or not. It's why I take the trouble to get properly dressed every day, despite the difficulties with buttons and hooks and zips and everything. I keep myself presentable. Unlike my friend, who turns up to lunch in her wheelchair wearing the same old nightgown that she wears when she lies propped up in her bed. It's white, more or less, if you look past the food stains down the front that the Vietnamese girl takes a sponge to from time to time. At the collar there's this faded line of embroidered blue flowers. What do you call them? Forget-me-nots.

My room is better than my friend's. There are trees in my window. Or bits of trees, at least. Leaves, branches, that kind of thing. On the floor below the window are potted plants that my daughter waters whenever she comes. There is a TV, hanging high up on the wall in one corner. And I have a whatsitsname, with pictures on it. Photos. There is also a big diary, open at today. My son writes in this diary whenever something is going to happen. I'm supposed to look at it every day, so that I know.

The pictures are of younger people mostly—children and boys and girls and so on—as well as one picture of an older fellow toward the back. Apart from the older fellow, they are all smiling, which is nice. The people on the TV are smiling too, which is annoying. They sit behind a desk with coffee cups in front of them and they talk and laugh and agree about everything, but they never look at each other. They look at me, or at the wall above my head. They seem happy, but that can change. Sometimes there are murders or politicians or people driving too fast in ridiculously large cars or serious fellows pointing at numbers. Sometimes people sing, or eat hamburgers, or sing while they are eating hamburgers, although I never have the sound on. Sometimes people play cricket for surprisingly long periods. At other times the TV stops moving altogether, and there are pictures of this place, with information along the bottom about what time lunch is on or bingo or a bus trip—the same sorts of things I am supposed to check for in the big diary that's always open there on the whatsitsname.

Whenever my son comes, the first thing he does, after pushing the picture of the older fellow toward the front of the whatsitsname, is to look at the diary, at the page it's open at. At the page at which it's open. At.

"Hello, dear," I say to him. I try not to sound surprised.

"You sound surprised," he says. "You have checked the diary, haven't you, Mom? It says that I'll be here today."

"Then I look forward to seeing you," I tell him.

He looks around the room, like he always does when he's not sure what I'm talking about.

But today my son also does something different. He looks at me with an expression I can only describe as sad. Rather than worried, impatient, constipated.

"Mom," he says, "are you okay?"

It is not possible to know what he means.

"There was a delivery today," I tell him. Was it today? I wonder.

"I could take you out for morning tea," he says, "if you'd like."

"Somewhere nice?" I ask.

"Of course. Somewhere nice."

"No thanks," I tell him, and he looks around the room.

Still, it's lovely of him to offer. He hates taking me out. Having to fold up my walker and put it into the what do you call it . . . the trunk, of his car. Having to fold me up too, to get me into the passenger seat, being careful with my head, then having to fiddle with the seat belt to make sure I'm safe, because my fingers can never manage the buckle thing. Having to find somewhere nice, having to explain the menu to me, having to worry about whether I'm enjoying myself. The poor dear, he is such a good son.

I tell him not to bother, we'll just ask the Laotian girl to bring us a cup of tea and a biscuit.

"My friend might join us," I say. "We could play Scrabble."

I don't know why I say this. My friend never comes into my room, and I never invite her. But he looks interested when I mention her, and I know he likes me to have whatsitsnames . . . interactions.

"She cheats, you know," I add.

Lunch in the dining room is meatballs, which means it is a special day. I don't ask. Maybe it's Melbourne Cup, although nobody has hats on. Nobody has a hat on. Or it's the end of the war again, or Christmas. The Angry Nurse is there in the kitchen, checking that the meatballs are gray enough. She is being angry at the Swedish girl.

I park my walker against the wall, under the big picture of the smiling sharks, and sit in my usual place. The sharks are in a swimming pool balancing beach balls on their whatsits. Snouts.

The fellow who doesn't live here is in the chair beside me, as usual. I say hello and ask him, as usual, whether his room is on this floor or on the floor below or on the one above, like mine. He looks admonished. Astonished.

"Oh," he says, "I don't live here."

"Oh, really?" I say. "Is that right?"

"I'm just visiting," he says.

"Of course you are," I say, and wait.

He looks around at everyone in their places at the dining tables, at the walkers and wheelchairs lined up against the wall. At the smiling sharks.

"I have a beautiful home," he says. "With a white fence and a two-car garage."

We eat our meatballs. The fellow who doesn't live here wants to tell me something. But I have offended him. He is always offended when you don't remember that he doesn't live here.

After a while he can't stand it anymore.

"Have you heard?" he asks me. He always knows things. For a fellow who doesn't live here, he knows a lot about this place.

I don't answer him right away. I look at the others around us in the dining room. None of them look like they know all that much. About this place or about anything else. I should be nice. The way they look at their plates, it seems that they are very keen to know everything there is to know about their meatballs.

"Heard what?" I say.

"The news."

"Sometimes. Not so much anymore. I don't like all the smiling."

"No. Have you heard what happened? Here, in this place?"

"There was a delivery," I tell him. He isn't the only one who knows things.

"Someone died," he says.

Then he tells me. Somebody fell out a window. One of the upper-floor rooms. Dead in the parking lot. He doesn't know all that much, but what he does know he knows with great pride. He whispers loudly. His eyes are bright. I think his hands are shaking.

"You must be very happy," I say.

He looks astonished again—offended again. What I have said is not what do you call it . . . applicable. Appropriate.

I go to my friend's room. Her door is open, so I look inside, but my friend isn't there.

"Hello, dear," she says.

I say the same thing to her. It's something my friend and I often do, even when we remember each other's names. I do it to my daughter too, and my son.

She lies propped up on the bed, facing her window. It's a different window from mine. Mine's better. Hers looks out over the parking lot; mine, of course, has the trees. There's one chair in the room: the same chair as in my room. It's right beside the bed. I sit on it, parking my walker alongside.

"Scrabble?" my friend says, as she always does.

Sometimes I ignore her, but today I don't.

"Why not?" I say.

"Why not, indeed?" she says, and reaches for it on the whats-itsname, knocking a photograph of someone or other onto the floor, as she always does.

"Fuck!" says my friend.

I tell her not to worry about it. The Malaysian girl will pick it up later, when she comes in to do the medication. My friend puts the Scrabble thing, the board, flat on the bed between us.

"What color would you like?" she asks.

"Black," I tell her.

"I think I'll have black too," she says, and gives me a handful of the whatsits with letters on them.

My friend and I play Scrabble for a while. We don't do it properly, and we don't care. She has her parts of the board, and I have mine. We don't build on each other's words, never share each other's letters, but we do praise each other's efforts.

"What word is that?" she might ask.

"Zbtosmty," I tell her.

"Most impressive," she says.

If one of us doesn't like a word, we grab the letters and throw them on the floor for the Peruvian girl to pick up later.

After a while, my friend decides that the game is over.

"I win," she says. "But don't be downcast, Rose, you put up a great fight."

"I know," I tell her. She always calls me by my name when she feels like showing off.

"See you at lunch?" she asks. "I think it's something special today."

We both laugh.

But I know my friend isn't here. I know that right now I am the only person in her room. I know that perfectly well.

My daughter carries the potted plants, one by one, from the carpet in front of my window into the bathroom, where she puts them in the bathtub. Each one makes her sigh as she moves them. As she moves it. Each potted plant is one more thing in her life.

"Are you sure you're okay?" she asks me.

She and her brother must have been talking.

"My friend fell out the window," I say.

"Try not to dwell on it, Mom," my daughter advises me. She doesn't need one more thing in her life.

I see her flying out the window. My friend, that is. The food-stained nightie with the forget-me-nots was not a very good parakeet, I imagine. Parachute.

My bathroom has everything you could want in a bathroom, as well as lots of things to keep you from falling down, breaking your neck and so on. Right now it looks like a jungle because of the plants in the bathtub. My daughter waters them with a plastic whatsit. It's the kind of thing she does. She worries that the pots will leak on the carpet under my window if I water them there. It's the kind of thing she worries about.

"You've had your medications?" she says.

"The Sicilian girl gave them to me. With a cup of tea and a biscuit."

My daughter looks annoyed. She doesn't like too much detail. She has a very busy life. There is already too much detail in it; there's no room for any more.

"I don't know if I can come tomorrow," she tells me. "Charity has a school excursion."

"Never mind, dear. How is she?"

"I told you before, Mom. She's struggling with biology."

"Poor darling. Education is so . . . important. How is . . . the other one?"

She looks at me, sighs. It upsets her when I don't remember things.

"Felicity, Mom. She's having some issues with work experience at the moment."

"What a shame," I tell her.

My window is a much better window than my friend's.

All through the dark night I lie in my bed, facing up to things. Well, it is dark, certainly. And I may be lying, obviously. And what I face up to, really, is the ceiling. Lying in bed, looking up, it's what I see. So I look at it. It offers very little of interest, but nevertheless. It is white, so it is something to look at in the night when everything else in my room is deep, dark shadow. The TV high up in the corner is an even deeper, darker shadow, having been turned off after my final medication. The whatsitsname with the photos on it is dark too, so you can't see all the smiling. The big diary is open, though you can't read it in the dark, and anyway it wouldn't be right to read about what it says is supposed to happen tomorrow until tomorrow.

In the window there is more darkness, unless there is a moon, but even if there is it is a long way away. Apart from the moon, there is one tiny light in the bathroom, so that you don't break your neck if you get out of bed to go in there. But why would I get up in the middle of the night just to go to the bathroom to break my neck?

Anyway, it's not the darkness. It's the time.

Time, in this place, is most unusual.

That's not true. In this place there is so much time, there's nothing unusual about it whatsoever.

There is no shortage of time here at all.

At night, in this place, you live forever.

Well, the night goes on forever, and being, to the best of my knowledge, alive, I go on with it.

Nothing happens, and it keeps not happening, then doesn't happen some more. It continues, and I continue with it.

Nevertheless. If you lie in bed in this place and listen, you can hear things beyond your own darkness. You can hear people breathing. Or not breathing, which is slightly more difficult. You can listen to them if you get sick of the ceiling. Sometimes you can hear them remembering, which sounds interesting but is even more boring than the breathing or the ceiling.

But what is strange about time, if not unusual, is that there are two different types of it.

There is the time that is endless. In this time, nothing happens. Nothing goes on, and it goes on forever. This is time that has insomalia. Insomnia. The only way to avoid it is to be asleep or dead, neither of which I appear to be.

Then there are the tiny bits of time that aren't endless. They do end; in fact, they end very quickly. Suddenly they are present, and then they are not. Except that they aren't present, whatever they are. What is present is the ceiling, obviously, and the insomnia.

I know what this second type of time is. Of course I do. These tiny bits of time are the past. They are from a long, long time ago. And yet.

It is the present that is long. It is the past that is sudden, and happens, and is present.

This is quite a pardalote. Paradox.

And here is another one. The endless dark present does finish, finally. The light comes, in the window. But you don't see it. Or you do, but before you see it you hear it. The sound appears in the window.

It is noisy. And it is now. And it is present.

And it reminds me of something.

S ometimes I wonder. Sometimes I wander. Me and my walker. My walker and I. We wander the polished corridors, where the nice boy who mops the floors is. Where the nice boy is, who mops the floors.

My walker and I ride in the thing, the revelator. Elevator. I am able to operate the buttons, which are big and bright, better than the buttons on my blouse. The elevator has a sign warning you not to use it if you are on fire. I am not on fire. I generally try to obey the rules.

I know my way around this place. Some of the time I am invisible and can go wherever I like. At other times I appear not to be invisible. I appear. I am smiled at. Or smiled at and scowled at, if it's the Angry Nurse. I am called *dear*. I am told I probably want a cup of tea. I am asked if I am looking for bingo. But when they're too busy or preoccupied or not in the mood, then I'm invisible and free to wonder wherever I like.

Of course, there are others in this place who do the same. Some of them are invisible also. Some of them like to be smiled at. Sometimes I smile at them myself, just to be nice. Some of them really are looking for bingo.

There are all different kinds in this place. Some different kinds, anyway. Some, like my friend, hardly ever leave their rooms except for meatballs or bingo. Some are silent, some always want to tell you things. Some tell themselves things, talking away at themselves as they sit in their wheelchairs lined up against the wall, deep in conversation with themselves, asking themselves important questions, like why are there wheels on their wheelchairs when all they do is sit there against the wall.

Whereas. Whereas I am free to wander. Up and down, in and out, as far as the big glass sliding doors that lead out to the parking lot.

I like sliding doors, when they slide. When they see you coming and they open, as if they know what you want. Others won't open at all, unless you know the whatsitsname. If you do know it, it's easy. The code. If you don't, then you are fucked, unless someone who does know it comes along and presses it in on the little Scrabble board thing beside the door and it opens, and then you and your walker slip through after them before the door closes, as if you knew the code all along but they just happened to get there first. This trick works more often than you'd think.

It doesn't work, though, for the big sliding doors at the main entrance. These are guarded by the Angry Nurse. She waits there in her office behind a vase of flowers and knows as soon as you get anywhere near.

"What can I do for you, dear?" she'll say.

The vicious, poisonous fury with which she says this is a miracle every time. Sometimes she'll go even further.

"What *exactly* can I do for you?" she'll say. And then she'll smile. You want to have good control of your bowels at these moments.

She is good at what she does, the Angry Nurse.

Today she is on the phone, and if I could I'd get out those big glass sliding doors and into the parking lot. But of course I don't know the whatsitsname that opens them, and there's nobody else around. There's nobody in the parking lot either. No body in the parking lot either. Except somebody's child folding somebody into the passenger seat of a car, being careful with their head, taking them somewhere nice for morning tea.

The Angry Nurse has seen me. She puts her hand over the phone, as though it's important to her that I don't see it.

"What exactly can I do for you, dear?" she warns me.

I'm not afraid of her.

"My friend isn't in her room," I tell her.

"Don't you worry yourself about that, dear," she threatens.

I don't say anything. I don't move. She hates that.

"What you need is a nice game of bingo," she says.

I would rather be pulled apart by horses.

"I'm sure that would be delightful," I say, and I look out again at the parking lot.

We understand each other.

My window is better than my friend's window. The window of my friend. The enemy of my enemy is my friend. The window of my friend is the friend of my window. Words are so . . .

My window is filled with trees. Close up and far away. So close that you can't see them; you can only see the leaves. And so far away that you can see the tree but you can't really see the leaves, just that they are green. Can't see the whatsit for the something or other.

It's the trees that I look at, when I'm not looking at the smiling pictures on my whatsitsname, or at the annoying TV. I don't know what the trees are. They are trees, obviously. I don't know what they are called. Trees. I don't know their names. It's not this that bothers me, exactly. It's that I love them. Which doesn't bother me. It's that I don't know why I love them, exactly. Or how, exactly, I love them.

I look at my window anyway, and I see the trees, and there is something. Something I love. Or something I remember loving, almost. I spend a lot of my time almost remembering. It doesn't bother me, not really. But there is something.

My daughter tells me it's nice that I have trees in my window. I tell her I don't know what *nice* means. What is this word, *nice*? I ask. Is it French? She tells me that I am being impossible and she doesn't have time for my games. She doesn't have time for trees either. My daughter knows nothing about trees. She knows nothing about potted plants, for that matter, except that they need watering and can ruin the carpet. And are another thing which she doesn't have time for. For which she doesn't have time. She is such a good daughter.

My son never looks at my window. He can't even see the trees. When he looks around my room the way he does, what he sees is what he pays for. Or what I pay for. Or what he pays for from my account, because he has the Power of Eternal. And every time he comes he moves the photo of the older fellow toward the front, for some reason. He is such a good son.

Sometimes, when he asks me what I've been doing today, I tell him I've been looking at my window. I tell him I hope that's all right, because it isn't written in the diary.

But when I look at my window, when I see the trees that are far away and the leaves that are close, there is something. I wonder about my friend's window. When she looks at her window, where there is a parking lot, is there something too? Is there something also? Is there also something? In my window there is certainly something. Or am I just being impossible?

My friend is not in her room again. Again, my friend is not in her room. Someone else is. A man. A man is in my friend's bed watching TV. Looking at it, anyway. He is on his back with his mouth open. He won't stay there for long, I suspect. Men rarely do in this place. Except for the fellow who doesn't live here, of course. When the fellow in my friend's bed is gone, perhaps my friend will come back.

I decide to ask the Doctor, or whatever he is, about it. I go and stand outside his office, which is near the office of the Angry Nurse. The door is open. He often says that the door to his office is always open, which isn't true, but today it is.

The Doctor, or whatever he is, is twiddling at his smart phone with his thumbs, the way young people do. I know what smart phones are. Felicity and Chastity are always twiddling with theirs, and you certainly get the impression that they are very smart indeed. The Doctor, or whatever he is, is very young. I'd say about fourteen. But he can't be, can he? He isn't at school, like Felicity and Chastity. He's here, and he's a doctor, or whatever he is. Unless of course he is doing whatsitsname . . . work experience. Like Felicity. Or Chastity. This is unlikely, I think.

When he sees me standing there in the doorway to his office, he smiles at me like he could eat me up. He is very handsome. He wants you to like him. He acts like he likes you.

"Rose!" he says, as if he is thrilled to see me and even more thrilled that my name is Rose. Some people use your name as though it's the answer to some terrifically hard question and they've got it right and won the competition and are already thinking about what they'll do with the prize money.

"People are falling out of windows," I tell him.

He smiles at me as if he loves me and as if I am very, very stupid.

"And there is a man in my friend's bed."

I see him think about making a joke. Sometimes he does that. He might say something about how good you look, if you're dressed up for Melbourne Cup Day or a bus trip, about how the fellows on your floor had better watch out. He'll make his eyes big, put on a witless grin, just about nudge you with his elbow to let you know you should laugh or at least see what a funny fellow he is. Except you can see he doesn't even think it's funny, he just thinks that you will. It's one part of his bedside . . . what do you call them? Manners. The other part of his bedside manners is when he talks to you straight out of some textbook, manual, that he has studied to become a doctor, or whatever he is. When he does this, he uses words like Individual. Care. Needs. Team. Feedback.

This is the way he decides to go now. After using my name one more time.

"Rose. You know our team here is committed to the highest level of Individual Care. Everything we do is in accordance with our Person-Centered Model. Integrated. Inclusive. Holistic. Best Practice. We value your feedback. If there's anything we can do to better meet your needs, anything at all. That's our Mission."

And he smiles as if I am the most beautiful thing he has ever seen.

I'm not.

He is very good at what he does. Whatever it is.

When my son comes, I am pretending to read the big diary. This makes him happy.

"It says you'll be here today," I tell him. This makes him look around the room the way he does. Then he goes to the pictures and moves the one of the older fellow toward the front. He fiddles with the thing at the back, the stand, so that the frame is sitting to his satisfaction. Standing. It's a nice frame. He doesn't say anything about it, just fiddles with it, and asks me questions about my medication and whether I'm eating properly. I give him all the usual answers.

The older fellow in the picture looks at me. I look at him. He is just a head and shoulders, and you can see he isn't wearing a tie. And he isn't grinning, so it's not one of those photos they take with their smart phones. Like Felicity and Charity, the way they hold out their smart phones at arm's length and grin at them and then show you the phone with a picture of them grinning.

There is nothing behind the older fellow in the picture, as there always is with Felicity and Charity. Like a mountain or an ocean or a crowd of their friends. Or in front of them, like a kitten or their dinner. Perhaps there is green around him, like leaves, as if he is somewhere near a window. The older fellow isn't grinning, isn't even smiling. He just looks at you. And what he looks like is that he is just about to laugh. As if he has just told a joke and is waiting for you to get it, and when you get it, he will laugh. Perhaps you will laugh too, or perhaps the joke is not that funny. It's hard to tell.

And there is something about his neck.

My son wants me to say something about the older fellow, I can tell. I don't say anything. My son tries to be patient. He's a good son. But he can't help himself.

"What are you thinking about, Mom?" he asks me.

What I'm thinking about is the ridiculousness of the question. That can't be a word, surely. How ridiculous the question is.

"I'm thinking about a game of Scrabble with my friend," I tell him. I watch him for a reaction. For some sign. For a clue.

"Your friend . . ." he says. Then he looks around the room.

I keep watching him.

Again, he can't help himself.

"Mom, I've spoken to the Care Manager. He's concerned about you."

"The Scare Manager?"

"No, Mom."

"That's good, then."

"No, it's not . . . Oh, forget it, Mom."

So I forget it. That's easy.

The nice boy who mops the floors is mopping the floor. I find him on the next level, near the end of a corridor, in the corner by a big double door with a sign on it. The sign says "Do Not Obstruct." The nice boy certainly doesn't look like he would ever obstruct.

He is always in a corner, or off to the side, or at the edge. He has a way of being there that is quite like not being there. It's one of the nice things about him. When he moves from side to side with his mop, he's always moving away as well. Even if he moves toward you, which he never does, he's always at the same time moving away or sideways or both.

He has short hair but with a long blond fringe hanging in front of his face like a curtain, or a mop. Really it is grayish blond, or ash blond, but still blond, closer to the color of his mop than to meatballs.

Which is strange, since the nice boy who mops the floors is dark. Felicity and Charity tell me I am not supposed to say that. It's not . . . appropriate.

"Nobody's dark anymore, Granma," Felicity tells me. "They're Black. You can't say dark."

"Or maybe brown—you can say brown," Charity informs me.

"Only if you're brown yourself," Felicity corrects her. "Otherwise it's racist."

Felicity and Charity know so much. They sometimes explain things to me when they visit, standing with their backs to the window and looking at their smart phones with their thumbs, while their mother waters my potted plants in the bathtub. They know all about the nice boy. Apparently he went to their school, but there were problems, so he is now on a special program.

"Probationary Work Placement," explains Felicity.

"Community Involvement Pathway," says Charity.

"Anyway, he's Black," they both agree. But when they say this, they both use those little marks in the air with their fingers around the word. Not the word *Black*. The word *he*.

The nice boy who mops the floors has a lovely voice. It is deep and soft at the same time, like a lovely private mumble, and it is impossible to understand a word he says. He has earrings in both his ears and in his nose and through his lips. Sometimes I think he has one in his mouth, stuck through his tongue. But that can't be right, and I can never get close enough to tell. He is gentle and mysterious and kind of folded in on himself.

"He's trans," Felicity tells me. "Or inter."

"And autistic," says Charity. "Or Asperger's. On the spectrum, anyway. Very, like, special needs."

They know so much. I understand so little of it.

The nice boy who mops the floors never smiles. He is never cheerful. He never asks how you are, or what he can do for you, or calls you *dear*.

"Something has happened to my friend," I tell him.

He says nothing, just mops. And sort of trembles, like water or leaves.

I realize I haven't asked him a question, so I try again.

"Do you know my friend?"

He says something. His voice isn't meant to be heard. It comes from somewhere deep inside him, and mostly stays there. He is polite, so he always answers. But his voice is a kind of silence. He swallows the words at the same time as he speaks them, so they come out sideways and broken and twisted, like little explosions that could even be curses. I don't take them personally. Sometimes I imagine he is saying nice things, like what a lovely blouse I am wearing. Or that he likes the trees in my window. Other times I think it might be *bitch*, or *cunt*. I don't care. Whatever he says is gentle and mysterious. I think he knows things.

"Do you know what happened to her?" I ask him.

He leans toward me, and at the same time shrinks away into the corner.

"Be careful" might be what he says.

Or it could be "Motherfucker."

The nice boy always makes me feel better.

My daughter arranges potted plants in my bathtub. Then she cleans the toilet, while I watch from the chair beside my bed. I tell her the Norwegian girl will do it, but she ignores me. So I ignore her when she asks me how my bowels have been.

Apart from my bowels, what my daughter is concerned

about today is Felicity. Or Charity. Felicity has lost her smart phone. Or Charity. Not lost it, really. Become separated from it. It is here: my daughter has it. Felicity or Charity left it in her mother's car on the way to school, then her mother came here to clean my toilet.

"She'll be distraught," my daughter says.

"Poor Charity. Felicity."

It is one more thing in my daughter's life. It takes her mind off my bowels. When she has finished cleaning my toilet, she describes for me the problem in all its . . . enormity. She could call one of Felicity's school friends and tell her to tell Felicity that she has it and will get it to her within the hour. Felicity's friends are all inside the smart phone, it seems. My daughter waves the smart phone at me so I can see. That would be the simple thing, though things in life aren't simple.

"Of course, it's locked, isn't it?" she asks me. It's a whats-itsname question.

"Locked?" I ask her back.

Rhetorical, that's it.

"Yes, Mom, locked."

I can tell from her voice that what she would like to say is, YES, MOM, FUCKING LOCKED! But she is a good daughter.

I try to help.

"How do you unlock it?"

"With the password, Mom."

"Password?"

"Yes, Mom, with the password." HOW DO YOU THINK YOU UNLOCK IT, MOM? WITH THE FUCKING PASS-WORD!

"What's the password?"

For a second, I think she might laugh. Or burst into tears.

"Mom. I. Don't. Know. The. Password."

"Why don't you call her and find out?"

This is fun.

My daughter has her own smart phone, and could call Chastity to find out her sister's password. Except Chastity is in an exam. And anyway, Chastity wouldn't know Felicity's password.

"The girls have been taught never to tell anyone their passwords."

"Is that right?"

"They've been brought up that way."

"Really?"

"You never tell anyone your password, do you, Mom?"

This is my daughter's small revenge.

"I wouldn't dream of it. Obviously."

When she has returned each of the potted plants from the bathtub to their place beneath the window, my daughter leaves to battle the traffic, as she always puts it, in order to go to the rescue of poor Felicity. Or Chastity.

As she leaves, she asks me if I have any plans for the afternoon. This might be a joke, although that seems unlikely. I tell her I might go and see my friend for a game of Scrabble.

The trees in my window, the pictures on my whatsitsname. When I'm not out wondering about this place with my walker, I look at the pictures or I look at my window.

Pictures. Window. These things are connected. I can see that. So, everything is connected. This doesn't help. Connected to what? To everything else? To itself? To its connection? To me connecting it?

Whatever, as Felicity and Chastity like to say.

My son and my daughter have brought in the pictures. I understand why. They are such good children. They like everything to be the way it should be. Nice photographs in nice frames. Some of the pictures are of Felicity and Chastity. My daughter brings them in, changes them, sometimes without my catching her. In some pictures, Felicity and Chastity are my granddaugh-

ters. Babies, side by side in a whatsit. A pram. A bassinette. Bassinette. A word you don't hear so much. Tiny pink toes. I can tell
them apart. Not the toes. Chastity and Felicity. Yes, in fact, the
toes. These toes Felicity's, these toes Chastity's.

In another picture, they are dressed up for a ball or something, in the sorts of dresses I sometimes see on the TV. All
bosom and glitter. Bosom. One of them is Felicity and one of
them is Chastity, I am led to believe.

There are pictures of my son and my daughter also, and
many other pictures. Of course, I know who they are. My son and
my daughter tell me so, often.

"Of course, you know who this is," they tell me.

But they never say it about the picture of the older fellow at
the back. They just move him more to the front, when they think
I'm not watching. At least, my son does. My daughter is too busy;
there are too many things in her life. I know that they are both
waiting for me to say something about the older fellow.

This is when I turn to my window. To the trees in it, and the
potted plants on the floor beneath it. Sometimes I ask my daughter or son to remind me of the name of a tree in the window or a
plant in its pot. But my son and my daughter aren't very good
with the names of trees or plants.

"Of course, you know what this one's called," I tell them
sometimes. I don't think they get the joke.

There is a man again in my friend's bed. Again, there is a man
in my friend's bed. He watches the TV. His eyes are open. His
mouth is open. Both, all, are pointed at the TV. Three smiling
people are sitting in a row behind a desk, being experts about
something with coffee mugs in front of them.

I move my walker closer. I hear him breathe. There is no
Scrabble board beside the bed, no wheelchair by the window.

The Nigerian girl comes in. She calls me Rose and says

good morning, so I back my walker away toward the door. She straightens the fellow's pillows, takes his pulse. His mouth stays open.

"He doesn't play Scrabble," I tell her.

She smiles at me and I go back out into the corridor, where the nice boy who mops the floors is mopping the floor near the "Do Not Obstruct" sign. He sees me and moves away toward a corner, his mop moving sideways with him over the floor. I watch the mop and the beautiful way the nice boy makes it move. Like a snake, like an endless figure eight, like some other symptom, symbol, that I don't know. I wonder something, and wonder if I've ever wondered it before. I wonder whether the way he moves his mop is a message he wants me to understand.

"I don't understand," I say. "Have you seen my friend?"

He looks terrified. Poor boy. I try to calm him.

"She fell out the window," I say.

He can't get any farther into the corner, so he speaks. Or at least he makes a sound in that beautiful voice that goes deep inside him as much as it comes out of him.

"Eternal love" might be what he says. Or it might be "Asshole. Fuck."

Just down the corridor, a sliding door slides open and the Angry Nurse comes through it, followed by the Doctor, or whatever he is. The Scare Manager. They go into my friend's room. I turn my walker around to follow them, but just then the Ukrainian girl comes past and asks me if I'm looking for bingo. By the time I've gotten rid of her, the door to my friend's room is closed. I knock and nothing happens. So I knock. Nothing happens. I listen. It's a thick door. The nice boy who mops the floors mops his way out of his corner and comes closer. I have the feeling that he's listening too.

"It's a thick door," I say.

"Love conquers all," he says. "Motherfucker."

Then the door opens, and we're too close.

"Rose!" says the Scare Manager, or whatever he is, beaming at me as if I'm his girlfriend or a movie star.

The Angry Nurse slips past him and comes straight at me, all threat and smile.

"What, exactly, can we do for you, dear?"

Neither of them bother, bothers, to look at the nice boy who mops the floors, cringing away into his corner.

I have to say something.

"My friend's wheelchair."

They smile at me as if I'm a kitten that needs to be put in a box.

"It's not by the window."

Or into a sack.

"It was by the window."

With a brick.

Time to go. I tell them I'm late for bingo but make sure I shuffle away with my walker slowly enough to overhear some of what the Scare Manager says to the nice boy, standing over him as he cringes down closer to his mop under the "Do Not Obstruct" sign. The Scare Manager doesn't bother using his . . . bedside manners. Not the jokes and the smiling, anyway. Only those words of his that sound like they have come out of some book that only the Scare Manager has read.

"Probationary period," I hear him say. "Conditional on. Performance, review of. Assessment, ongoing. Monitoring, continual. Interactions, problematic. Benchmarks, professional. Feedback, constructive. Team Player, be one."

The nice boy gives no sign that he understands these words any more than I do. He doesn't make a sound. His curtain of mop-colored fringe hangs down low over his face and his mop makes little twitching movements on the floor, as if it's alive and suffering. Or as if it's trying to send me a message that I don't quite get.

My son is a good son. My son understands the value of things. He knows what this place costs. He is very good with numbers. Sometimes he talks to me about my account. Apparently I have one. He tells me I can check it anytime, if I wish. But I need to use my pin.

"My pin? Like a needle?"

"PIN. Like a password."

"I see. Like Felicity's. Like Charity's."

"Well, I suppose." He looks around the room the way he does. He has already moved the picture of the older fellow to the front of the whatsitsname.

"I could use Felicity's password. Or Charity's. Then I could check my account."

"No, Mom. It's your own. Nobody else's."

"Nobody else's?"

"That's right."

"But you know it?"

"Yes, of course. I know it."

"You could write it down here in the big diary. Then I could check my account. And I could get through the sliding doors by myself."

"Through the . . . ? No, listen, Mom—it's very private. Nobody else can know it."

"Nobody?"

"That's right."

I look at my window. There are trees. He is a good son. He buys me things. He has bought me Scrabble. He puts the box on my bedside table. He takes it out of the bag to show me. It's not . . . what do you call it? Gift-wrapped. That is not necessary. My son is very practical.

"What's that?" I ask him.

"It's Scrabble, Mom."

"Scrabble?"

"Yes. You used to play it with your friend."

"My friend?"

"Yes, Mom."

"Used to?"

He looks around the room.

At dinnertime, the dining room is as it always is. Smiling sharks on the wall. Wheelchairs and walkers lined up against the wall beneath the sharks. Everyone sitting in their place at the table, staring at their meatballs. I join them, getting myself into a chair and letting the Sri Lankan girl take away my walker and put it against the wall, beside the wheelchairs, beneath the sharks.

The fellow who doesn't live here is in his place beside me.

"Which level are you on?" I ask him, because I know he likes me to.

"Oh, I don't live here," he tells me.

He speaks about this for a while, then he stops. He seems to want to talk about something else.

"I have a password," I tell him. "Do you have a password?"

But this isn't what he wants to talk about. He wants to talk about the Scare Manager or whatever he is.

"The Scare Manager?"

"Care Manager."

"That's what I said."

He wants to talk about him, anyway. About how he has a new car. He seems to think this is important. An expensive new car. He talks about what type it is. The names and numbers and all that. I ask him if it's the sort that people drive very fast through rivers or along the beach or right up to the edge of cliffs for a picnic, like the ones I see on my TV. But now he's talking about a watch. A very expensive watch, he tells me.

"It's a Rolex," he says, as if the word is secret and special, like a password.

I think he has trouble keeping to one subject.

I wonder where the nice boy who mops the floors is. Where the nice boy is, who mops the floors. I think about the Scare Manager, or whatever he is, talking to the nice boy who mops the floors about being a team player, and the nice boy's mop squirming on the floor at his feet like a frightened animal. And the way the Scare Manager jabs his finger at the face of the nice boy and says Probationary. And the big shiny gold watch I see on his wrist as he says it.

"How does he afford a watch like that?" asks the fellow who doesn't live here.

"Who? The nice boy who mops the floors?"

He gives up on me and eats his meatballs.

I go into my friend's room. Perhaps I feel like a game of Scrabble. My friend isn't there. There is a man in her bed.

Of course there is.

I move my walker close to the bed, look into the man's face.

He does nothing, just breathes and stares at the TV.

I study him closely.

I don't like him. His hair is silver, like the older fellow in the picture on my whatsitsname. But this fellow is nothing like that fellow. His mouth is open, as if by accident. Like an unbuttoned . . . what do you call it? Fly. Not as if he is about to say something. The older fellow in the picture always looks at me as if he's about to say something. Or has already said something and is waiting for me to laugh. This fellow doesn't look at me and isn't about to say anything and would never make anyone laugh. And there is something about his neck.

"What is your password?" I ask him.

He doesn't say anything.

The sound is off on the TV, just like mine. A young woman is reading the news. Or selling something. Or telling jokes. The man in my friend's bed watches the young woman with his mouth open. Or perhaps he doesn't. Perhaps he is looking at the window. There is a parking lot in the window. But no wheelchair beside it. He isn't going anywhere.

"My window is better than yours," I tell him. Why should I be nice? "All you have in your window is a parking lot."

He breathes. He stares with his open mouth at the TV. He understands me, I think.

"My friend was in that parking lot. On her back, looking at the sky. Her wheelchair was there by the window."

The Brazilian girl comes in.

"Rose," she says. "I see you've made a new friend."

"Yeah, right," I almost say. It's what Felicity and Charity would say. Or else, "As if." Or, "Whatever." Or just, "Not."

I look at him again before I leave the room. He breathes and stares with his mouth open at the TV or the window or the parking lot. And there is something I don't like about his neck.

But I think he understands me.

My daughter takes the potted plants from beneath my window and places them in the bathtub. Then she waters them with a plastic watering thing. Can. Watering can. Watering plastic. She does this with great care and with great sadness, because Felicity, or Charity, has failed her whatsitsname. Driving test. Just because while she was behind the wheel she got a call on her smart phone and answered it. The call was from Charity, or Felicity, wanting to know how the driving test was going. She said it was going really well, that she'd done a perfect hill start and reverse park.

"But then the driving test guy goes ballistic," says Felicity. "You can't do that, he says, like I can't take a call on my own phone."

"Creep," says Charity.

They both stand by the window, their backs to the trees. Their eyes and their thumbs never leave their smart phones when they speak. They are very good at letting you know they are not really here.

My daughter finishes watering the potted plants and starts cleaning the bathtub. When she finishes this she will wipe over the toilet seat, then come out of the bathroom and begin dusting the pictures on my whatsitsname. She will sigh as she does all these things, and talk about how she will now have to pay for more driving lessons, book another test, find the time to drive Felicity and Charity everywhere they need to go, as well as get to work herself and somehow manage to come here and attend to my potted plants and bathtub and toilet seat.

"It's not as if the potted plants will get into the bathtub by themselves," I point out.

"Exactly," she says, and sighs.

My daughter moves the picture of the older fellow toward the front. She doesn't look at him, just wipes his frame like it's another thing in her life. She puts him down, sighs. There is something.

"Mom," she says.

"Yes, dear?"

Felicity's and Chastity's thumbs are blurs of movement. Nothing that happens in this room, even if something were to happen, could ever . . . what's the word? Imperil, impugn, impinge on them. Upon them.

"Mom. Are you? Worried about? Something?"

My poor daughter. She doesn't need this in her life. Me being worried. She is too tired at the very thought of it even to sigh.

"The Care Manager is concerned," she says.

"The Scare Manager?"

She looks at me. She doesn't want any of my nonsense. Felicity, or Chastity, gives a little laugh, like a snort, but probably at her smart phone.

"And what is he concerned about, dear?"

"He's worried about you, Mom. He says you seem. Unsettled."

"Unsettled?"

"He's afraid you're becoming confused."

"Afraid? Confused? Becoming?"

She looks at me. I could keep this up forever.

"He's worried that you are upsetting the other residents. And the staff."

"Upsetting them?"

"Mom."

"Sorry."

"He says you're being a nuisance. Annoying people."

"I see. Did he say anything about Feedback? Best Practice? Person-Centered Models?"

She's impressed. But still tired. And annoyed.

"How about Inclusive? Holistic?"

"Mom. We all know what you're like."

I resist the temptation to ask her. Until she and Felicity and Chastity have gone. Then I ask myself.

What am I like?

I am supposed to regularly consult the big diary for information about what will happen tomorrow, or today if I can manage to wait that long and handle the . . . suspense. Not that anything happens today, of course. The diary is about the future. It is about looking forward. Although sometimes there is nothing there either, as if tomorrow has been canceled or . . . reprioritized. At these times, and even though the diary is all about the future, I often find myself turning back pages and looking at previous tomorrows.

This can provide all kinds of interesting information, about when things had not quite happened, and what day it was, whether it was a Tuesday or a Thursday, or sometime before Melbourne Cup Day but after the fall of Rome.

Here is an earlier day, for example, when there was to be a bus trip. This is never quite as exciting as it sounds, but nevertheless.

Getting everybody onto the bus takes almost as long as waiting for the day of the bus trip to arrive, and then the bus takes an awfully long time to get to where it is going so that it can turn around and come back again, after which it takes even longer for everybody to get off the bus than it did for them to get on.

And never, no matter how many times you ask the fat bus driver, will the bus drive very fast into a river and then out the other side, like you see cars doing on the TV. But at least you can look out the windows or at the back of the bus driver's head, and perhaps somebody will fall out of their seat or lose control of their bowels, so that everybody comes back tired and happy.

Or else there is the day when the Easter egg hunt was to take place in the dining room, which was sometime between the Crucifixion and the Resurrection, apparently on a Friday. This promised to be a lot of fun, because things were to be hidden, which is not unusual in this place, but there was to be some sort of reward for finding them, which is.

However, seeing all those poor souls in their wheelchairs and food-stained nighties fighting each other to be the first to get the treasure, and looking for it behind the picture of the smiling sharks or concealed inside a toilet bowl, does make you wonder about people.

And here is the day when the war ended again, and there were flags and old songs about bluebirds going over cliffs and about how we'll all meet again, and some fellow turned up wearing a soldier's uniform, which excited some of the old dears here and frightened others.

So the big diary certainly can be useful. It may not exactly fill the time, but at least it does provide another way for it to happen.

I look at my window. Beneath my window, on the floor, there are plants in pots. In my window, up close, there are leaves. Beyond the leaves in my window there are trees. I don't know what they are. They are trees, obviously. My window is a better window than my friend's.

My friend and I play Scrabble in her room. My friend cheats. She lies propped up in her bed, facing her window.

"What word is that?" I ask her.

"Zbtosmty."

"Most impressive, dear."

Then she tells me something.

"I don't like the Doctor," she says. "Or whatever he is."

"Of course you don't, dear."

"He scares me."

"Scares you?"

"He comes in here, into my room, and smiles at me."

"Horrible."

"He tells me I look like a million dollars. Says if he was fifty years younger, and laughs."

"That's what he's like."

"He tells me he has a plan for me."

"A plan?"

"A Scare Plan, he says. He tells me it's an Individual."

"Person-Centered?"

"You know him."

"I don't like him either."

"He frightens me."

My friend looks at her window. There is a parking lot in it.

My window is better than my friend's. I look at it, the green, the leaves, the trees. I don't know what they are. That's the problem. No it isn't. It's the window. I can look at it, but that's all. I can look at it, but not through it. Or not into it. It's a wall. It's a screen, like a TV. A screen I can look at, but not into.

It doesn't upset me. Not exactly. What is it I feel? A need?

Surely not a desire. I have everything I need. And I have no desires. Is it a loss that I feel? A lack? Alack! There's a word. A word. It's always a word I lack.

I think they might have changed my medication.

The Scare Manager and the Angry Nurse come into my room, smiling, to tell me that they have changed my medication. He has a gold watch, a golden chain around his neck, a golden earring, possibly a golden tooth. He tells me how good I look. Tells me that the fellows on my floor better watch out. Tells me that if he was a few hundred years younger, or something. And smiles. The Angry Nurse smiles too, which is even worse.

He tells me it is a Medication Review. Individual. Person-Centered. The Angry Nurse does the work with the papers and labels and her whatsitsname . . . clipboard. The Scare Manager does his bedside manners, his words that come from somewhere entirely different from where other words come from, somewhere where words are careful not to attach to other words or to things. I wonder what he'd be like at Scrabble. As he talks, he looks around my room as if he has never seen it before, as if it is the best of all possible rooms and it exists entirely because of his words, his bedside manners, the smile that never leaves his face. As if it is Individual and Person-Centered.

"It's all about Feedback," he says to one of the potted plants. "Continuous Monitoring and Assessment of Individual Needs. Evaluation. Reporting. Reviewing. Reevaluation. Recalibration. Going Forward."

The Angry Nurse lifts up my foot, looks at it, puts it back down, writes something on her clipboard. Number of toes, perhaps. Evaluation. Reporting.

The Scare Manager talks about my Satisfaction Levels.

"My Satisfactoriness Levies?" I say, but the Angry Nurse smiles, so I stop. I don't want her picking up my foot again.

"We're all members of a team here, Rose," the Scare Manager warns me.

"Are you happy here?" asks the Angry Nurse, as if she's wondering whether I'm using my incongruence pads. Incontinence pads.

"Happy?" I say. "Happy?"

The Scare Manager looks disgusted at us both for using such language. He picks up a photo and looks at it as if it isn't there.

"We're passionate here about our Model of Care," he says.

"When's bingo?" I ask him.

He looks at me. He smiles. He puts the picture back down on my whatsitsname. He picks up another one. His bedside manners keep dribbling out of him while he does these things, leaking from him absentmindedly like into an incontinence pad. He can't be bothered making whole sentences. He'd prefer just to throw me out the window. He says something about his Core Focus. About Commitment. Shared Vision. Continuous Quality Improvement. Best Practice. Integrated. Holistic.

It's the photo of the older fellow he's holding now. He looks at it. It's a nice frame, although it isn't gold. He runs his fingers over it. He turns it over, looks at the back as if there might be something there.

I don't like him holding that picture, looking at it, touching it. The older fellow looks out of the picture with that serious expression of his as if he is about to say something funny, even as he's spun around and fiddled with by those absent-minded fingers oozing their bedside manners. I'm not sure what it makes me feel, seeing the Scare Manager handle that picture of the older fellow the way he does. It makes me feel something. Ownership? Protectiveness? Fear? Rage? Whatsitsname?

"Something happened to my friend," I say.

The Scare Manager smiles.

We understand each other.

I flip back through more pages of the big diary until I arrive at the most recent tomorrow on which my son was to take me somewhere nice for morning tea.

There were all the usual difficulties with getting my walker into the car and then getting me into the passenger seat while being careful with my head and then all the business with seat belt buckles and finding a place to park and all the other things that make my son hate taking me anywhere nice for morning tea, but once we get there and I have ordered a lamington, my son looks very proud of himself, which is pleasant to see. One of the things that makes him proud is that from the café he has taken me to I am able to see the sea.

I am glad that this makes him proud.

I don't like the sea.

From the café you can watch people walking along the water's edge with their dogs. I don't particularly like dogs either. There is one that the Angry Nurse allows into this place from time to time, in order to cheer everybody up. To cheer up everybody. It is a cute, cuddly chimera. Chihuahua. It is a horrible little thing.

Anyway, I don't like the sea. I suppose there's probably a reason for that, like drowning. I don't even like the seagulls, which always want your lamington. I like completely different birds, somewhere else, nowhere near the sea.

Although I must say I quite enjoy the penguins. They are big and fat and waddle around the water's edge like bus drivers and have long necks and enormous beaks and always look like they are about to say something funny, or else swallow someone's Chihuahua.

My son, on these occasions, likes us to have what he says is a conversation. As there is no diary for him to consult or pictures for him to rearrange, he sometimes talks to me about his investments. Or even, occasionally, about his wife and son. His son, who has finished school and now has investments of his own and so, of course, no longer comes to visit his grandma. And his wife, who no longer comes either. The last time she ever visited, she got quite upset for some reason, and mumbled very loudly to herself that I was an impossible old cow, which almost made me like the bitch.

Anyway, my son and I have a conversation, while I have a lamington. This often involves him telling me what I was, and what I know.

"Of course, you'd know all about that," he might say, "having been a teacher."

"Education is the future," I'll say, because he likes to hear this kind of thing.

I don't ask him what I taught or who I taught it to. To whom I taught it.

The truth is that I don't much like people telling me what I was. I'll decide what I was. Perhaps I was an astronomer. Or a sailor. Or an investor, or a bus driver.

Whatever.

I have spent some time studying the big diary more closely. I
know it contains important information. Not just what my son
may have written about what is to happen tomorrow, or the tomorrow after that, whether he might be coming to take me somewhere nice for morning tea or whether that Chihuahua is coming
for a visit to cheer all of us up. To cheer up all of us.

I know that the purpose of the diary is to tell me what is
important. I know it is designed to tell me what is happening.
To tell me what is going on.

But it has another, secret purpose. Which is to tell me what is
happening. To tell me what is going on.

There are things in the diary which I have written myself.
They are secret things. It is important to have secrets. I have
hidden these things in the past. I have turned back pages to previous tomorrows, and I have written down things that I have
learned, from either my own explorations in this place or else
what my friend has told me, based on her own research. And I

have hidden them here and there in the diary. I have hidden them so well that they cannot be found. Which is perhaps unfortunate.

I know they are here somewhere. Perhaps here, near the day when we were about to have the quiz night, which was memorable because, as far as I remember, nobody got a single question right, despite all the cheating. Of course I know all about cheating, having been a teacher. Or an astronomer or whatever.

I keep looking. I keep turning pages. I know there are things here about things I have come to know. About what happened to some of the poor souls here that something happened to. There is something about injections. Somebody was given an injection of something, and it was the last thing they were ever given. Somebody else was found hanging from something, and it was definitely the last thing they ever hung from. From which they ever hung.

I am almost certain that there is something about somebody with a plastic bag over their head. And somebody else had their neck broken, although that could have been my friend.

I know they are here but I can't find them. That's how I know they are important.

Right here, between Labor Day and the defeat of the Ottoman Turks at the Battle of Lepanto, which if I am not mistaken was a Sunday. Right here there was something.

I know it was here because it is gone. So I know it was important as well as here. It was a cue. A clue. It was right here on this page. Which is not here. Which has been removed.

The whole page has been torn out of the diary.

Which is interesting information.

With my walker I go wondering, wandering, looking for the nice boy who mops the floors.

I think he knows something.

For a long time I don't find him. I make my way along corridors. There are others with walkers, others in wheelchairs. I don't like any of them. My son sometimes lets it be known that I might take greater advantage of the opportunities for companionship in this place. I tell him I don't like bingo. Or I tell him I would like bingo if it wasn't for the numbers. I shouldn't be so difficult, he tells me; he only wants me to get full value out of this place. And what, he says, it has to offer. My son knows about value. And numbers. And offerings. It upsets him to think that I don't whatsitsname myself of what is available. Avail.

What I liked about my friend was that she was always in her room, almost always in her bed. I never bumped into her in corridors. I don't like bumping into people. Not bumping, really, of course. We all move slowly enough that there are seldom any collusions. Collisions. Instead, what you get are slow approaches along corridors, slow hopeful approaches with slow hopeful grins on each side, and witless looks as each side attempts to remember, or wonders whether there is anything to remember. I hate it when they try to remember. When they look at your face as you approach along the corridor and grin at you as if this might help them remember, or might fool you into thinking they remember, or that you might remember for them and then everything will be wonderful. I hate all this remembering they try to do in corridors. It's not . . . dignified.

I have to wait at the sliding doors on the next level. I hang about, looking natural, until the Argentinian girl comes along and puts in the password and the doors slide open and I follow her through.

The nice boy who mops the floors is mopping the floor beneath the "Do Not Obstruct" sign, looking different. Or not different so much as more the same. More silent, more retreating sideways as he moves his mop over the floor, more trembling like leaves in a window. His fringe of blond hair looks longer and more blond. Which makes his skin look darker. Or would do if that was not racist.

I move closer to him. He retreats, he trembles. He has more

earrings in his lips and eyebrows. And perhaps in his tongue, but that couldn't be right.

It's good to see him.

"They changed my meditation," I tell him, for conversation. "Medication."

"I've missed you," he says in his beautiful, silent voice. Or, "Piss off," possibly.

"Who is the man?" I ask him.

Perhaps he asks what man, perhaps he doesn't.

"In my friend's bed."

His mop curls and coils on the floor like a cornered creature. I won't let him get away. He shrinks, he retreats, he goes sideways, but I follow him. His silence grows; he hides inside it. I wonder if he might disappear, if he might be able to make himself invisible. But I won't let him. He makes a sound. A curse, or a threat, perhaps. But at least we're getting somewhere. Then he says something else.

"Do you run and play?" I think he says.

This seems unlikely, so I ask him again. "Who is he?"

"Someone who can pay."

I'm almost certain this is what he says.

"Shit," he adds. "Fuck."

This makes him feel better. He looks at me, more or less.

"Be careful," he says. "You're in danger."

Then he says, "Asshole. Motherfucker." But this is only to make me feel better.

At least he doesn't smile at me. He never smiles. It's one of the things I like about him most. One of the things I like most about him.

My son looks surprised. He is reading the big diary.

"What is this?" he says, and looks at me.

"It's a diary," I tell him.

"I mean what's written here. Who wrote this?"

"Well, it's my diary, so I suppose it was you."

"Mom. It says here: *I am in danger*."

"Oh, that. That's my password."

"No it isn't, Mom."

"I wanted to remember it."

"Remember what?"

"The danger."

"Mom, there is no danger. You're safe here. You do feel safe, don't you, Mom?"

"Feel?"

"Who told you that you were in danger?"

"Told me? Somebody."

"Well, it's not true."

"It must be true."

"Why must it be true?"

"It's in the diary."

The conversation goes on like this for a while, but I lose interest. I look at the leaves in my window. I wonder about the man in my friend's bed. He can pay, the nice boy said.

"It's about money," I tell my son. My son understands money.

"Money?" he says.

"Exactly. I knew you'd understand."

"You don't need to worry about money, Mom. You have money. In your account."

"Not my money. Other people's money. And gold."

"Gold?"

"Gold. It's a precious whatsitsname. Metal."

My son's face has a very serious look, which it gets whenever he talks about money or thinks that I might be going mad.

"What money, Mom? What people?"

"My friend. And the man in my friend's bed. And the Scare Manager."

"The Care Manager?"

"That's right. The Scare Manager."

My son looks around the room, fiddles with the pictures,

moves the one of the older fellow toward the front. I look at the leaves in my window.

"Always wipe your bottom thoroughly," I say, I hope not aloud. Training him to use the . . . what do you call it? The potty. Then, when he was bigger, the proper toilet bowl, once he could climb up onto it with my help. My good, serious son, very serious about his toilet training, a very serious look on his face as I help him pull down his pants.

"Always wipe . . . what did you just say?" he says, with a very serious, comical look on his face.

Whoops. You never know when you might say something out loud. You need to be careful.

"It's my password," I tell him.

The leaves tremble in my window. In my window, the leaves tremble.

It's the breeze. People in this place like to talk about the breeze, about the temperature, about the weather. There is very little weather in this place, but they like to talk about it all the same. There is weather in my window, and sometimes it makes the leaves tremble. Or shine. Or . . . glisten. Up close, and far away. Farther away, anyway. Close. Closed. Close and close. Words are so. They have their own weather, and it changes, whether or not. My medication has definitely been whatsitsnamed.

The picture of the older fellow has once again worked its way toward the front. He doesn't smile. I like that.

Beyond the leaves are trees. Beyond. I know what they are. What trees they are. I am almost sure I know.

Why do I look at the picture of the older fellow, as if he might help?

Camellia japonica. Azalea indica.

What are these? Are they passwords?

The older fellow in the picture looks at me, not smiling. But about to laugh. Or about to make me laugh, perhaps. Above his collar there are lines on his neck. Like bark on a tree. Or, now I look more closely, not lines but spots. Spot the spots.

Corymbia maculata.

Passwords? Past words?

Whatever they are, they return. Perhaps I should write them in the diary.

There is something wrong with the fellow who doesn't live here. Over meatballs, I ask him which floor his room is on, and he tells me.

"This one," he says. "I live on this one."

"I'm so sorry," I tell him. It is, perhaps, the saddest thing I have ever heard, although I couldn't be certain.

He looks around the dining room. The sharks are smiling and balancing their beach balls, the wheelchairs are lined up against the wall. The Angry Nurse is shouting at the Inuit girl in the kitchen. Everything is as it always is.

"Everything is changing," he says.

"But your double garage? Your beautiful white fence?"

"They've changed my room."

"Changed?"

"It's not my room."

That's more like it. That's more like the fellow who doesn't live here.

"I loved my room," he says. "I miss it."

This is too much. I try to snap him out of it.

"But you don't live here, surely?"

"Not for long. Not without my room."

"Eat your meatballs," I suggest. "You'll find them quite unusual, since you don't live here."

"They've changed my medication," he tells me.

"Oh dear. That can't be good."

"My TV is different. My bed is different. My window is different."

"Your window? I have a window. You can use mine."

He looks at me.

"Everything is changed. My room. My account. My password. I don't recognize any of it."

"I have an account," I say. "And a password. You can use mine."

But I can see that he doesn't believe me.

"I love . . ." he begins, then he stops. I don't know what he loves. I don't know what I love either, for that matter. Perhaps I should put my arms around him, give him a hug. Perhaps I should give him a kiss.

He looks at his plate.

"These are not my meatballs," he says.

At least there is that.

I go to my friend's room. I take Scrabble along with me. There is a man in my friend's bed. I don't like him. But I need to speak to him.

His eyes are open; his mouth is open. Also, his pajamas are open, which is not pleasant.

I sit beside him and put the Scrabble board on the bed between us.

"What color do you want to be?" I ask, but he doesn't get the joke. He might be looking at the TV high up on the wall. There's nothing on it but a disaster somewhere. He might be looking at his window. There's nothing in it but a parking lot.

My friend always cheats at Scrabble. I miss her throwing the Scrabble whatsitsnames on the floor when she loses. I miss her praising my efforts and what do you call it . . . patronizing me after she has claimed victory with a word that doesn't exist.

Words that exist, words that don't exist. There are words that don't exist, but are. There are words that exist, but aren't.

"You can be white," I tell the man in my friend's bed. "I'll be black. And white."

The disaster on the television has turned into a man leaving a building, surrounded by a crowd with cameras and microscopes. Microphones. The microphones are on long poles and are covered in fur like small, unhappy animals that are stuck in the face of the man leaving the building. The man is perhaps a criminal or a politician, or perhaps he is an innocent man just trying to leave a building. The man in my friend's bed looks at the man leaving the building, or possibly at the window, with his mouth open. And his pajamas.

I make a word for him on the Scrabble board and show it to him.

"Pig," I tell him. "Well done."

Then I make a word on my side of the board and read it to him.

"Qzpwokxlafely," I say. "That's two hundred and forty-seven points."

I build another word for him on top of his first word. I give him my most patronizing smile, even pat his arm.

"Dog. You're doing so well. I can see I'll have to keep my whatsitsnames about me. Wits."

We go on like this for a while. I cheat, I patronize, I chat about my friend. From time to time I throw the Scrabble things on the floor, for realism. He just lies there, but I'm reasonably certain that he is annoyed, irritated. Possibly enraged. I give his arm another pat. There are lines on his neck that I don't like the look of at all.

"I bet you have money," I say. "I bet you can afford to pay. I bet you have an account with lots and lots of money in it. I have an account too, with fabulous amounts of money in it. But probably not as much as you. Is that right? I bet you can afford to pay more than anybody else, can't you? But I have a password. Do you have a password? Of course you do. I bet nobody else knows your password, do they?"

He just looks at the TV with his mouth open. Now there's a comedy show on. You can tell because everyone takes turns to laugh at each other. I'm not sure how I know that he is a bad person, but I do. Not just because he is in my friend's bed. Not just because his mouth is open, and his pajamas, or because of the nasty lines on his neck.

"Of course nobody knows your password. How could they? Unless. Perhaps. Perhaps there is somebody. Perhaps, somehow, somewhere, somebody does know your password. Do you think that could be possible? Do you think that right now someone somewhere might be using your password? Typing it in on one of those little . . . pianos? Keyboards? To get into your account? Your very own personal password? Your very own account? Just imagine that. Goodness me, those lines on your old neck are nasty, aren't they?"

Those lines are nasty all right. Nasty and red and angry, as if his throat has been cut.

A shadow fills the doorway. It's the Angry Nurse with her clipboard. I smile at her before she can do it to me.

"We've been having a lovely game of Scrabble," I tell her. "But I must be off. Time for bingo."

Charity and Felicity are here with their smart phones. My daughter wants to know about my bladder. She worries about me having a bladder infection. Bladder problems can cause other problems, she tells me. Cognitive Dissonance, she says. I wonder where she got this. From the Angry Nurse? The Scare Manager?

"How is *your* bladder?" I ask her.

"Mom," she says.

"How is *your* bladder, Felicity?"

Felicity actually looks up from her smart phone.

"Ooh," she says. "That's gross, Granma."

"How about *your* bladder, Chastity?"

"Charity," says my daughter.

"Whatever," says Chastity.

There's nothing wrong with my bladder. I'm not so sure about my Cognitive Discotheque.

"I remember when I used to wash you," I say. "You liked to pee in the bathwater."

Nobody says anything. Nobody is sure who I'm talking to. To whom I'm talking.

"You had the pinkest little toes," I tell them, and it's true. I'd wash them one by one, as well as between them, with the whatsitsname, and count them as I went, making up a little rhyme about each one. And they'd giggle. Not the toes, obviously. The granddaughters. And the daughter. And the son, for that matter. So many toes.

The older fellow in the photo watches me as I think these things. He doesn't smile, but might be about to laugh. Somehow he has worked his way to the front again. Did I ever wash his toes? It seems unlikely. But those spots. On his neck. *Maculata*. Nice, pink spots, nothing like the nasty red lines on the neck of the man in my friend's bed. I wonder if the older fellow has a password. He doesn't really look the type. But, then, everybody has a password, don't they?

My son looks confused. He is about to move the older fellow to the front of the whatsitsname, except he's already there. Because he's confused, he looks at the open page of the big diary for comfort. My son likes to know what's what, and when.

"I think it's Melbourne Cup Day," I tell him. "Or it's my birthday, or the war has ended again."

"I don't think so, Mom," he says, but I think he knows I'm only trying to help.

"Bingo, then? A bus trip? Or quiz night?"

He looks around the room.

"Rhododendron," I say, because I feel like I should say something.

"Excuse me?" he says.

"Of course. But do you know what it is?"

"What *what* is, Mom?"

"Rhododendron."

"Well. I think. It's a flower. Isn't it?"

"I see."

"You'd know, anyway."

Would I?

He looks around the room again. Then he goes over and picks up the picture of the older fellow. For a moment it looks like he might push it toward the back, which would be a first.

"Perhaps it's my password."

"Motherfucker," says the nice boy who mops the floors. I'm glad that he wants a conversation, but I'm worried about him. He doesn't look well. His fringe is longer and dirtier, and his mop barely moves on the floor. It just lies there, as though it's ill or tired or has a bladder infection.

"Do Not Obstruct," says the sign.

"I have leaves in my window," I tell the nice boy. "You'd like them. They tremble."

"Beautiful," he says. Or, "Bullshit," or something.

"The thing is, I seem to know what they are. They have names. The trees, I mean."

He has been crying. He might even be crying now.

"Port wine magnolia," I tell him. "*Michelia figo*. Weeping bottlebrush. *Callistemon viminalis*."

"What?" he says, or "Shit," or "Prick," or "Cunt."

"They're like passwords."

I have never asked the nice boy who mops the floors whether he has a password. I'm almost sure he does. He knows about secrets, I am certain of that. Perhaps he is entirely made up of passwords. But perhaps he doesn't know what they are. Perhaps everything he says, or almost says, is a password. Perhaps his passwords are so secret that even he doesn't know what they are. Perhaps he, himself, is a password. Could you be a password and yet not know what the password is? It's a whats-itsname. Convolvulus. Conundrum.

"I'm worried about you," I say, and move my walker a little closer. Perhaps he is like the older fellow in the picture. Perhaps both of them are passwords.

I decide to tell the nice boy some things about the older fellow. I don't know if they're true, but he seems interested. Or afraid. I suppose they are true, since I say them.

"He has these spots on his neck," I tell the nice boy. "I quite like them. Not like the lines on the neck of the man in my friend's bed. Which I don't like at all. The lines, not the bed. I like your earrings, by the way. Have I told you that? I even like your mop."

This may be too much. His mop trembles, twitches. I must be more careful. I don't want to frighten him. That's interesting. The nice boy who mops the floors is someone I don't want to frighten. The things you find out.

But it isn't me, I, who has frightened him. The sliding door has slid open and here comes the Scare Manager, with the Angry Nurse and the Transylvanian girl. They come straight at us, all smiles and bedside manners. The nice boy lets out a little sound. It might be "*Fuck*." It might be "*Help*." It might be "*Please save me*."

The Scare Manager comes right up to the nice boy, looks as if he might touch him. The nice boy backs away toward the "Do Not Obstruct" sign. This doesn't help. The Scare Manager follows him, and looks right into the curtain of the nice boy's fringe as if he knows everything about him. I wait for him to say something about Holistic, about Person-Centered, about Best Practice.

But it's worse than that.

"Go to my office immediately," the Scare Manager tells the nice boy. "We need. To discuss. Your situation."

The nice boy's mop dies, right there, on the floor at his feet.

The Angry Nurse smiles.

Since the nice boy varnished, vanished, I've been spending more time in my window. At my window. Through my window. The trees, the leaves. Leaves. I leave, you might say. Words are so. I leave, and I am in the leaves. Here I am in my room but somehow I leave my room, I leave the potted plants on the floor beneath the window, I leave the big diary open at today and the picture of the older fellow on the whatsitsname, and I leave. I find myself among the leaves. Among. I am among the leaves, and I find myself.

Or perhaps it is a bladder infection.

But I know their names. These leaves, these trees. Surprisingly enough, there are words for them all, like passwords, and I seem to know what they are. Hibiscus. Lilly pilly. Crepe myrtle. *Brunfelsia grandiflora*. Yesterday-today-tomorrow. Kiss-me-quick. And Rose, of course.

And here I am, among them. I am present, and so are they. There is a presence. Presents. It is a gift, this presence. Words.

But something beyond words. Beyond this window. Beyond the present. But present. A presence.

I should tell my daughter about this.

My daughter looks at me.

"What?" she says, a potted plant in each hand, on her way to the bathtub.

"I said I seem to believe in God."

"You? Believe in God?"

"Yes. Why didn't you tell me that I believe in God?"

"Because you don't, Mom. You never have. It's me. I believe in God. Remember?"

I hate it when she tells me to remember. What does she think I'm trying to do, for God's sake? But she's the one who gets angry. Which looks comical, with her arms full of potted plants. She says she's the one who believes in God. She says that's why Felicity and Charity go to the school they do. She says that's why she does what she does.

"Oh, I see. That's why you put the potted plants in the bathtub?"

She looks at me.

"I believe in God," she says. "You don't. All right?"

She is very angry. And very tired. Having to explain all this to me is another damned thing in her life.

"Well, I'm glad we straightened that out," I tell her.

I don't tell her about the presence among the leaves.

I wonder the corridors with my walker. Wander. There are "Do Not Obstruct" signs, but there is no nice boy mopping the floor. I ask the Macedonian girl if she knows anything about him, but she just seems confused. Or frightened. Or perhaps she has a bladder infection.

And the fellow who doesn't live here is nowhere to be seen. I look for him at dinner. There are meatballs. There are the smiling sharks on the wall balancing their beach balls. But no fellow who doesn't live here. I tell a woman at the table beside me that I suspect she might have the wrong meatballs. This gives me some pleasure. She looks at me. She tries to remember who I am. You and me both, I tell her, and she looks around the dining room. I tell her I'll see her at bingo.

And my friend is not in her room. She liked to call me Rose, for her own reasons. To get an advantage. She cheated at Scrabble. Rose. She never called me Geranium. Or Petunia. Or Daffodil. Or *Myosotis scorpioides*. Forget-me-not.

There is a man in my friend's bed. His mouth is open, and quite possibly his pajamas. I don't wish to look. He stares with his open mouth at the TV high in the corner. Or possibly at his window. There is nothing in that window but a parking lot.

M y son wants to talk about money.
I know my son wants to talk about money because he has written about it in the big diary. I don't know when he wrote it, but there it is. *Mom, we need to talk about your account*, it says. Perhaps he wrote it last time he was here. Perhaps he snuck in here and wrote it in the diary when I was asleep. Snuck. Perhaps he sneaks in when I am asleep and dreaming about. Something. Perhaps he sneaks in here when I am sleeping and dreaming, and he writes in the big diary and moves the picture of the older fellow to the front of the whatsitsname.

I shouldn't say he sneaks. My son is a good boy. He wipes his bottom thoroughly. He believes in. Not God, like my daughter, but other things. Not just money. Taking care. Keeping track. Getting value. Incomings, outgoings. These are things he says sometimes, when he is looking around the room and I am looking at the window.

"Mom, we need to talk about your account," he says.

"I have a password," I tell him.

"Of course you do," he says, but nothing more.

"It's my own. My very own. It's private. It's personal. Nobody but me knows it. Nobody knows it but me."

He looks around the room.

"Nobody in the world. Nobody in the whole wide world."

"Well," he says. "Mom," he says. "I know it," he says. "I know it, of course. You know that, Mom."

"You know my password?" I look astonished.

He looks at me looking astonished. He looks at me carefully. Careful. Full of cares.

"You trust me, Mom, don't you? Everything I do is for your benefit, you know that."

"Trust? Benefit? Know?"

I shouldn't do this to him. But he sneaks in here, moving my pictures, writing in my diary, knowing my password, with his thoroughly wiped bottom and his careful look. Sometimes it makes me want to make him look even more careful, even more full of cares. Still, I shouldn't do it. I am a cow, and I am impossible.

"You're a good boy, son," I tell him. Then I say: "Aren't you?" I can't help myself.

He looks around the room. I pretend to look at my window.

"Well. Mom. We need to talk about your account."

"Let's talk about my account," I say, trying to help.

"You may notice some changes."

"In my account?"

"When you check in to your account, yes."

"With my password?"

"Exactly."

Exactly.

So, he talks about my account. He says there are a few small changes. I make a joke about small change. He doesn't get it. He says he's talking about minor adjustments. He says he's talking about routine restructuring. About monitoring and evaluating. About continual improvements to ensure something or other, going forward.

"It's funny," I tell him.

"Funny?" he says, afraid I might be about to make another one of my jokes.

"Funny how you sound just like him."

"Him?"

"Exactly. The Scare Manager. Exactly like him."

He looks at me even more carefully. And. What? Nervously? Guiltily?

Anyway, he looks at me, so I look around the room. There's the older fellow in the picture, right at the front of the whatsitsname. The older fellow isn't smiling, but he looks likely to laugh at any moment.

"*Gardenia magnifica*," I tell him. My son, not the older fellow.

"*Gardenia magnifica*," I say again, because I like the sound of it. "That's my password."

"No it isn't, Mom," says my son, and looks around the room.

Gardenia magnifica. I look at my window, and I am in a garden. It is what do you call it . . . magnificent. And I am in it. I am . . . present. But, also, there is a presence. It is not God, apparently. I am holding the picture of the older fellow. And I am in a garden. And the older fellow is here, beside me. Present.

Everywhere there are whatsitsnames. Plants. Bushes. Shrubs. Trees. They are beautiful. They have beautiful names. And there are beautiful spots on the older fellow's neck. *Corymbia maculata.* Spotted gum.

I know this place. I know the beauty, and I know the words. Words. Beauty. Perhaps I am a poet. I must ask my daughter. Or perhaps not.

The older fellow is here beside me. We are here in this garden, side by side, and it is magnificent. And there are words. Words pass between us. Passing words. Passwords?

Words pass between us, but I can't quite hear them. They

are present, but I can't quite here them. I can't quite make them here.

I must tell someone. I wander with my walker, looking to tell someone. Something.

My friend is not in her room. There is a man in her bed. The nice boy is not mopping the floor, even by the "Do Not Obstruct" sign. The fellow who doesn't live here is not in his usual place in the dining room.

I follow the Assyrian girl through two sets of sliding doors and, since I am not on fire, I take the revelator down to the lower floor and find myself by the main entrance looking out on the parking lot where my friend was delivered, on her back in her nightgown with the forget-me-nots. Well, I don't really find myself. What I find is the Scare Manager, in his office with the Angry Nurse. The door is a little bit open.

They are fighting. Arguing, anyway. I can tell this by the way they smile at each other, and whisper.

"I can count," I hear the Angry Nurse say. Or, "Account."

The Scare Manager tells her that everything is. Under. Control. I can hear that his mouth, his teeth, his smile, are all whatsitsname as he says it. Clenched.

The Angry Nurse tells him he needs to be very. Very. Careful.

I see her in her Angry Nurse's uniform lean at him over his desk. This frightens him so much that he laughs.

"You concentrate on your bedpans," he tells her. "Leave the numbers to me."

I feel her smile. Very quietly, she tells him to think carefully about something or other.

"Bingo!" I say.

It's beautiful to see the way their heads turn, together, as if they're on the same neck. Then they smile at me, both of them.

"Rose!" says the Scare Manager, too loudly.

"What can we do for you, dear?" says the Angry Nurse.

You need to be careful at moments like these. Keep it simple.

"Is this the way to bingo?" I say.

But it doesn't work. They look at me, both heads smiling. Then they look at each other for a second. Then they look at me. Then they ask me to come in.

I tell them I'll be late for bingo, but they smile. I move my walker through the office doorway slowly, as if I am very old, very helpless, totally harmless. I don't fool the Angry Nurse one bit. She comes at me.

"Let me help you there, dear," she says, and puts me into a chair by the Scare Manager's desk.

"Don't you look wonderful?" he tells me.

"I am full of wander," I say.

The Angry Nurse is behind me, where I can't see her. She could kill me with a single blow.

"You look like a million dollars, Rose," he says, and since I know where this leads, I try to help him.

"The fellows on my floor need to watch out," I say.

But this is too much. Not only does the Scare Manager laugh, too loudly, but behind me the Angry Nurse laughs too. It is a terrible sound.

"Rose," the Scare Manager says. "Are you happy here?"

I look at him.

"I am very fond of the meatballs," I say.

"It is important to us that you are happy," he says.

"And safe," the Angry Nurse says behind me.

"And comfortable," he says.

"Comfortable," says the Angry Nurse. Or possibly, "I'll kill you all."

"You know that, don't you, Rose?" the Scare Manager says.

"I know all kinds of things," I say. I can't help it.

He smiles. Or is it a laugh? Just a little one, but he's worried.

"What do you know, Rose?" he asks, and I can feel the Angry Nurse move closer behind me.

"Things are being changed. Things . . . varnish. Vanish. Other things return. Disappear. Reappear. People are no longer here. Others come back."

"You trust us, Rose, don't you? You need to trust us."

"Trust?" I say. "Us?" I say. Ah, it's an old game, and I'm sick of it.

"I seem to know words," I say. "Past words."

"Passwords? What passwords, Rose?"

The Angry Nurse breathes, behind me.

"My friend's nightgown. When she was delivered, in the parking lot. There were flowers around her neck. They were *Myosotis scorpioides*."

"Really?"

This doesn't interest either of them. I must try harder.

"The man in my friend's bed. The fellow who doesn't live here. The nice boy who mops the floors."

Silence.

"There is something. About money. About accounts. About passwords. Something."

I wonder if anyone saw me come in here. If anyone in the world knows I am in here with the Scare Manager with the big gold whatsit on his arm. Risk-watch. Wristwatch. With the Angry Nurse behind me, breathing.

I could so easily varnish. So quickly disappear.

"Or perhaps I have a bladder infection."

"I know things," I tell my daughter.

My daughter sighs. She is so tired.

"Of course you do, Mom."

"Things are changing," I say. "Things are being changed."

"Nothing is changing," my daughter says, putting a potted plant in the bathtub. She says something else I can't quite hear. Perhaps it's: "Nothing ever changes."

"Don't be afraid of change, Granma," says Charity, or Felicity. God bless her.

"Change is good," says Felicity, or Charity. Neither of them looks away from their smart phone as they say these things, but still.

My daughter keeps on putting potted plants into the bathtub. She is so helpful. So busy. She is so busy being helpful, it's hard to get her attention.

"My password . . ." I begin, then I stop, leaving her space to finish for me, to be helpful and impatient, to tell me my password out of sheer tiredness and busyness.

"What about it?" she says finally. So, no luck there.

I try something else.

"Your brother," I say.

Nothing.

"Your brother knows my password."

She picks up another potted plant.

"Just hold it with that *Monstera deliciosa* for a second," I tell her.

This gets her attention, so I keep going.

"Your brother sneaks in here and he pushes the picture of the older fellow to the front of the whatsitsname."

Now I've lost her again.

"Then the next thing I know, I'm in my window and I'm holding the older fellow in the picture. I'm holding the picture of the older fellow."

She stops with the potted plants. She looks at me.

"Mom, he was the same age as you."

I have no idea what she's talking about.

"Ancient," says Felicity.

"Poor Granma," says Chastity.

"Poor Second Grandad," says Felicity, or Chastity.

They're very talkative today. I'm not sure I like it.

What I do like are the spots on his neck. *Maculata*.

In the sun. Sun spots.

I sit in my window with the older fellow in the picture. In my window, I sit with the older fellow, in a sunny spot.

The sun shines on us both, and we are in a garden.

We are in our garden. Side by side, with the sun shining on us. And on the spots on his neck.

"This is our garden," I say to the older fellow.

"It certainly is," he says.

"I like those spots on your neck," I tell him.

"Of course you do," he says very seriously, or at least without smiling. "They're my best feature." And he laughs.

This seems entirely reasonable.

In our garden, with words passing between us.

Blueberry ash. Ivory curl. *Elaeocarpus reticulatus*. *Buckinghamia celsissima*. *Brunfelsia grandiflora*. Yesterday, today, and tomorrow.

Passing words. Past words.

The nice boy is here, not mopping floors. From the dining room I see him in the kitchen with a thing on his head. He is in there with the Babylonian girl, who is wearing the same thing on her head, and they are doing something with trays of food on the bench beside the . . . sink. Perhaps they are removing the color from the meatballs.

The thing on the nice boy's head, the hairnet, hides his beautiful hair, his lovely mop-colored fringe. It hides his hair so that he can't hide behind it, but he manages to hide anyway. He shrinks, he closes, he shuts, like a flower that shuts its petals tight at the end of day. *Tulipa clusiana. Gazania tomentosa.*

I try to get his attention, but he makes himself smaller, closes himself tighter. More tightly. I don't give up. I call out.

"Where is your mop? What have they done to your mop?"

The Babylonian girl smiles at me. Perhaps the nice boy looks my way for a second, then he hides himself among the meatballs.

I look around the dining room for a witness, and there in his usual place at the table, under the picture of the smiling sharks with their beach balls, is the fellow who doesn't live here, looking insoluble. Inconsolable.

I move my walker over to him, slide onto the seat beside his, and give his shoulder a little pat. He knows what I'm thinking.

"Here I am," he says.

"Why isn't the nice boy mopping the floor?" I ask him, since he always seems to know things.

"Everything is changing," he says.

"Change is good," I tell him, but he doesn't believe it any more than I do.

"You've seen his new car?" he says.

I know who it is that he's talking about.

"I've seen his risk-watch too," I tell him.

"He changed my account," he says. "My password. My room. My window."

I wonder if he might cry.

He looks like someone who has never seen a garden in the sunshine.

They are such beautiful spots. *Maculata*. On his neck, in the sunshine, in the garden. Our garden.

"Our garden," I say, just to check.

"Our garden indeed," he says. "Our very own garden."

Am I wrong to think he squeezes my hand as he says this? As we sit, side by side, in the sunshine, in our garden?

Yet he is an older fellow, I'm sure of it. Despite what my daughter says. The same age as me? God knows what that is. And Felicity and Chastity. Second Grandad? God knows what they're talking about.

God, perhaps.

And he squeezes my hand. In the sunshine, in our garden, holding each other's hands.

His touch. In this place, I am no longer touched. Except

when they sit me up higher on my pillows, or when they give me my tea and wrap my fingers around it as if I don't know how to hold a cup and sorcerer, or when the Algonquin girl feels for my pulse to see if I'm dead. And it is never like this touch. In this touch, something moves. Something flows. Something flowers.

In the sunshine. In our garden. With the flowers. Flowing. Flowering. Flow. Flower. Words are so.

And there are roses. Rosaceae. Rosa. Rose. Our roses.

Floribunda. *Mutabilis*. Crepuscule.

Pierre de Ronsard. Wollerton Old Hall. Albertine. Iceberg. Fearless. Seduction.

There are roses, and there is sunshine, and they are the same. Something flowers. Something flows.

And there are birds. The older fellow and I sit side by side in our garden with the flowers all about, and the birds. They are all about us, always. Always in flight, in the sunlight, and always making their bird noises. Chattering, chuttering, chittering. Calling to each other, talking to each other. They never stop. They are always talking and squawking, asking and answering, bird words passing between them that I can't what do you call it . . . translate. And I don't know what they're called, for all their calling. And I don't know the words that pass between them. I have no words for them or their words, but they are always flying, moving back and forth in the air like breathing. They never stop, so the garden never stops, the air moves and flaps and flies and squawks and screeches and asks and answers, and the roses bounce and tremble when they land and when they fly off to other flowers, and everything flowers and flows as they follow each other and their words pass between them in the air like sunlight, like life. There is life, and it is all about us.

And there are beautiful red spots on his neck, like roses. Rosy, like roses, liked by Rose. Ring around the Rosie.

He squeezes my hand. And there is a ring on my finger, on the hand that he squeezes.

Ring around the Rosie. Pocket full of whatsitsnames.

We are the same age, apparently, and we are like children.

The words of the birds pass back and forth, and they are all about us in the air, in the sunshine.

And there is love. The older fellow squeezes my hand and the ring on my finger and he says: "I love you, Rose."

And then the birds are so loud. The noise of them bursts and blossoms and is all about us, and I wish I knew their names. Kookaburras. Laughing kookaburras. But they can't all be kookaburras, and as well as laughing there is screeching and trilling and squawking and talking and chattering and chuttering and the sound of them all is as bright and blossoming and bursting as the flowers and somehow they become one flower, one rose, and then I realize it is one bird. I know that, impossible as it is, all this noise comes from one bird, one bird making all these words, and the words have in them all the birds and all the flowers and all the sunshine and all the roses as well as the one Rose. And then I know that it is not these things at all that are making the sound, that are saying the words. It is me and I am speaking, and not even all that loudly, but the noise of it is everywhere and everything.

"And I love *you*," I say.

O h" is what my son says when I tell him I'm in love. And: "Is that right?"

"I don't know if it's right. What I know is I'm in love."

Later I say the same thing to my daughter.

"I am in love," I say.

My daughter says nothing.

"Go, Granma!" say Chastity and Felicity.

I ask my daughter the same question I asked my son.

"Why didn't you tell me I was in love?"

"Mom," says my son when I ask him, and looks around the room. I see him see the picture of the older fellow, which is not at the back of my whatsitsname, or toward the front near the big diary. It is in my window, where I left it. On the whatsit . . . the sill. Above the potted plants. *Deliciosa*.

"I'm glad," he says, but glad is not exactly what he looks. Glad. Gladiolus. "Of course you loved him."

"Loved? What do you mean, *loved*?"

As for my daughter, if she notices the picture of the older fellow in my window, she doesn't say. My daughter is very good at what she does.

"Why didn't you tell me?" I persist. That's what *I'm* good at.

Eventually, she weakens. "*Love, love, love,*" she mumbles, aiming the words at the bathtub. And sighs.

Well, fancy that. I'm in love. I'd like to tell my friend, but she fell out her window. Perhaps I will tell the fellow in my friend's bed.

I still don't like him. I sit beside my friend's bed and I look at him. He looks at the TV. His mouth is open, and his pajama pants.

"Guess what?" I say. "I'm in love."

A fly lands on his face.

"Not with you, of course." It's important that he understands this. "I don't like *you* at all."

The fly crawls across his face. I wonder why it is that I don't like him so much. That I so much don't like him.

"You can't even play Scrabble," I tell him.

But that's not the reason, not really.

That he is in my friend's bed. That my friend isn't. That he has enough in his account to be there, and my friend hasn't. Doesn't. That he has a password. So he can just lie there looking at the TV with his pajamas open, and a fly crawling over his face.

"You're not so special," I say.

The fly looks into his mouth, thinks about going in. It must be nasty in there.

"Your account could be changed, like everyone's."

The fly decides against it and crawls toward a nostril.

"Maybe they know your password."

The fly doesn't like the look of things in there either.

"Maybe *I* know your password."

The fly moves down toward his nasty-looking neck.

"I know all sorts of passwords. Passing words. Past words."

Those nasty-looking lines on his nasty neck. They are red, but not rosy. They look like they've been made with a knife, or at least by something sharp, but without quite cutting through. Like they've been . . . scored. Score along the dotted line. His score. Words are so.

The fly walks along one of these lines and its little legs disappear inside, as if in a furrow. A trench. A score line.

The lines on the neck of this nasty fellow in my friend's bed.

The spots on the neck of the older fellow in the picture.

These nasty. Those not.

So then, this is why I don't like the fellow in my friend's bed. Not only because he can afford to be lying here, in my friend's bed, but because the lines on his neck are not the spots on the older fellow's neck.

More than that: it is because he is not the older fellow.

Still, here he is. With his mouth open. And his pajamas.

And something else.

For the first time, I understand that this fellow is older than the older fellow.

So why is it that I think of the older fellow as the older fellow?

Older than what? Older than who? Whom?

This seems to be important, somehow.

Yet I don't have time to wander about this right now. I can hear the Scythian girl approaching, bringing tea or medicine or meatballs.

I wait as long as I can, because the fly is on the move again. I watch it crawl back up to the edge of the fellow's nasty mouth, then go inside.

"Bye for now," I say. "Enjoy your fly."

O lder than what? Older than whom?

Perhaps my son knows. My son knows so many things.

So I write a question in the big diary for him to see the next time he comes.

"What's this?" he asks when he sees it.

"It's a diary."

My son looks around the room.

What I have written is a simple enough question, I would have thought. And yet my son, although he knows so much, is easily confused.

What it says is: *Who is the older fellow older than?*

I try to help him.

"This older fellow in the picture. The older fellow that you always move to the front of the whatsitsname . . ."

"Dresser."

"Dresser? What sort of name is that? German? Austrian?"

Now he's even more confused. I am such an impossible cow.

"Anyway, whatever his name is. Let's not worry about names. This older fellow. He is older, obviously. Older than . . ."

My son just looks at me with that same worried look he gets when I talk about accounts and passwords. I need to make it easier for him.

"Let's start again," I suggest. "This older fellow, whatever his name is. I am in love with him."

My son looks very tired. As if he has been spending too much time organizing things, handling things, dealing with things, looking after my account. But I can feel that I'm close, so I say it again.

"I love him. Don't I?"

"Of course you do," he says, as if he has given up.

"Of course I do. And he is . . . ?"

"He's your husband. Was. He was your husband, Mom."

Now we're getting somewhere.

"So he's my husband. And he has lovely spots on his neck. And I am in love with him."

My son looks even tireder than he did before.

"Your father," I say, and he kind of . . . winces. As if I've just thrown something at him, or said *fuck*.

"No," he says. "Your husband." And he looks around the room.

All these things are connected, of course. Of course they are.

I don't care so much about names. It's more about time. For the first time, I find that I care about time. For the first time in a long time, I care about time.

It's about time.

Ha-ha.

There is the picture of the older fellow on the window. Sill. He doesn't smile, and he has lovely spots on his neck. And behind him in the window there are trees, and through the window there are more trees, and flowers, there is a garden, there is the noise of birds, there is the sound of *I love you*.

And over there on the whatsitsname are all the other pictures. Younger pictures, smiling pictures. I look at them and I see lots of smiling, and lots and lots of time. They are family pictures, obviously. The Dresser family.

I look at these pictures closely.

I like the frames particularly. They help the pictures stand up, which is a good thing, and they show that the pictures are important; important enough to be put in a frame. A frame with flowers around the edges, or little hearts, or seashells or angels. In fact, there are more different types of frames here than different types of smiles in the pictures inside the frames. Because, in fact, smiles all look pretty much the same after a while. In fact.

But here's one frame that isn't standing up. Here's one at the back that has fallen down. Fallen over onto its smiles. I stand it up again on its what do you call it . . . stand, and I look at it.

There are two babies. They are smiling. Giggling, really. More importantly, they are wiggling their little toes. More importantly, someone is standing behind the two giggling babies. Or bending over them, from behind, and tickling them, making them giggle and wiggle their toes. More importantly, this someone is a man.

More importantly, the man does not have a head.

More importantly still, there are lines on his neck.

I know those toes.

I know that neck.

The toes are not the toes of Charity and Felicity. These are the toes of my son and the toes of my daughter.

The headless man is their father.

He is tickling his babies' toes.

The headless man is my husband. But he is not the husband I am in love with.

He has lines on his neck.

My daughter is carrying potted plants into the bathroom. In a
moment she will find the picture in the bathtub.

Here she comes now, holding the picture. She puts it back on
the whatsitsname. It would seem that she intends to say nothing
about it.

"Nice picture," I say.

She has returned to the bathtub with two more potted plants.
She is silent, but the way she kneels beside the tub makes it clear
that she is too busy for my games.

"It is you," I say. "You and your brother."

She is silent.

"And a man without a head."

Nothing.

"Interesting that he has no head, don't you think?"

Still nothing. She thinks she can keep this up for as long as
I can.

"I wonder who took off his head?"

But she can't.

"You did," she says. "You did, Mom. You did."

"I don't like those lines on his neck," I say.

She manages to say nothing.

"I should have taken off his neck as well."

I suppose that's no way to talk to my daughter about her father.
But I really don't like those lines. Or the way my daughter kneels
by the bathtub, as if she is saying a little prayer.

"You don't think he could be the fellow in my friend's bed?"
I ask her.

"In your friend's bed?" she says. And sighs. And puts her
head down on the edge of the bathtub. When she lifts her head
again, she does it very slowly. She is very, very tired.

"He is dead, Mom," she says.

"Dead? The fellow in my friend's bed? Perhaps he swal-
lowed a fly."

"My father," she says. "Your first husband."

My first husband?

I look at my window. At the picture of the older fellow that sits on the windowsill. Beside it I place the picture of the dead fellow who has no head. I need to classify a few things. Clarify.

My first husband. My dead first husband. My headless, dead first husband.

And the older fellow. Who is in the garden through the window. Beyond the window. Who is beside me in the garden, in the sunshine, with the flowers. And beside me in the garden he says, *I love you, Rose*, and there is the noise of the birds. And in the noise of the birds there is the sound of me saying, *And I love you*.

Okay. All right. So, here is the thing.

There are two husbands.

There is an older one, who is dead. And who has no head. And who is the father of my children.

And who is younger than the older fellow, who is in the garden beyond the window, and who I am in love with. With whom I am in love.

Also, the older, headless one, who is younger than the older fellow, has nasty lines on his neck and yet is not the even older fellow in my friend's bed.

I must put all this in the diary.

I go looking for the nice boy who doesn't mop the floors. I wish to talk with him about love.

He isn't in the kitchen, where the Sumerian girl is folding ser-vitudes. Serviettes. But as my walker and I move away through the empty dining room, past the smiling sharks, there he is. In a corner. He has no mop.

Instead, he holds a tray of what might be mashed potato, which he tries to hide behind as I approach.

Someone has cut his hair. He has no mop, and he has no beautiful, mop-like fringe to hide behind. All he has is the tray of what might be mashed potato. All of us in this place are familiar with the mashed potato, and if there is one thing we agree on it is that it might be mashed potato. Some of us have wondered what its secret whatsitsname, ingredient, might be. It occurs to me now that it might be mop water. I must concentrate.

"I am in love," I tell the nice boy.

"Get fucked," I think he says. It is so nice to talk.

He has less earrings. Fewer earrings. Mainly in his ears. They don't exactly sparkle. At most they give off a dull . . . glimmer.

"But something is wrong," I say.

"Cunt," he says. Possibly. When he says a word, he seems to swallow it at the same time as spitting it out. Which is not unlike the mashed potato.

"Something about words. And remembering."

There is something else about the nice boy. He appears to have breasts. Not exactly a bosom, but nevertheless.

I need to concentrate.

"Something about rooms, and windows."

He looks at me from behind the mashed potato. I think he knows things.

"And accounts. Something about my account."

"Fuck it," he says.

Exactly.

"Fuck, fuck, fuck," he says.

Exactly. Exactly. Exactly.

Except he's not talking about what I'm talking about. He's talking about the Angry Nurse, who is approaching along the corridor with her clipboard, smiling.

"Better head for the hills," I say, and that's what we both do. In our very different ways and in at least two different directions, we make a run for it. It must look quite comical. But it doesn't feel funny. We manage to get away, we manage to escape, but only because the Angry Nurse doesn't come after us. She must have something better to do with that clipboard.

But I can't help thinking that something *is* coming after me. Something that I can't get away from, and that I won't escape.

T hen the next day, or the next month or year or something, the nice boy comes to my room. I am in my window when I see him approaching. I am with the older fellow, there is a garden and flowers and there are birds, and there are the lovely spots. And there at the same time, whatever time that is, there is the nice boy and he is coming along the corridor toward my room and toward my open door with its piece of silk on the door handle. Not exactly straight toward it, of course. There's plenty of sideways as well, as if he still has his mop. But I can see him from my window, and he is definitely approaching, although not definitely, exactly, but in that way of his that is anything but definite and looks less like advancing than retreating, or something.

Nevertheless, he somehow gets to the door. And he sees the piece of silk on the door handle. I look at him looking at it. There he is, without his mop or his mop-like fringe, but with his surprising breasts and those earrings in his eyebrows, and he is close enough to touch that piece of silk.

Which is exactly what he does. He feels it, with his fingers.

What else would he feel it with? With what else would he feel it? I see him, from my window, and it feels as if he does not see me seeing him. I wonder whether I am not visible to him. In fact, I wonder if I am invisible, there in my garden with the sunshine.

And yet, the nice boy looks at that piece of silk as if he is . . . recognizing it. As if he is recognizing me.

And I watch, invisibly, as he feels that silk with his fingers. So gently. So . . . what? Feelingly.

Lovingly.

The way he loves that piece of silk between his fingers, the way he . . . caresses it between his finger and his thumb. It reminds me of something.

It reminds me of Charity and Felicity, the way they hold their smart phones, so tenderly, and the way their thumbs move so surely, so knowingly, with such understanding.

The nice boy understands something.

But I appear to be invisible. Or I am not visible; I do not appear.

And as if the silk has filled him with courage as well as love, and as if he can't see me, he comes into my room. Withdrawing and advancing at the same time, but coming into my room, nevertheless.

He looks around my room, the way people do, but he does it as if he doesn't want to look, as if he doesn't want to see. Or is it that he doesn't want to see *me*? Even though I'm invisible? Anyway, moving forward as well as backward and sideways, the way he does, he somehow gets as far as the big diary lying open on the whatsitsname.

Which is where he stops. Or stops stopping, and goes right up to the diary and looks at it. Reads it, I suppose. Then picks up the pen. He must know I'm there, watching. But he pretends that I'm not, so I can pretend that he's not there either. So we can both pretend that he isn't holding the pen in his hand and isn't about to write in the diary.

Which is not all that difficult, since the way he writes in the diary is entirely different from the way my son writes in the diary. The nice boy writes something, but he writes the way he speaks, the way he moves, the way he mops floors. Doing and not doing. Advancing and retreating. Not exactly forward, not exactly backward, not even sideways, exactly, so much as appearing to look for a different way altogether.

But he does write something.

Then he puts down the pen and moves backward and sideways toward the open door and, beyond it, to the corridor along which he will make his escape, all the while hiding behind his nonexistent mop-like fringe. His lovely fringe, the color of a nonexistent mop. Making himself, as much as he can, invisible, if not entirely nonexistent.

Invisible. Nonexistent. Two related things, although not entirely the same. I appear to be invisible in my window, while I appear to exist in my garden. In my perhaps nonexistent garden. Where I exist, to say the least, with the flowers and the birds and the older fellow and the love, nevertheless. Even though I haven't yet read whatever it is that the nice boy has written in my diary, he has given me much to think about.

He has almost made it out the door, to the corridor into which he will disappear.

But then, what do you call it . . . apostrophe. Catastrophe.

In the doorway is my son. Not exactly catastrophic in itself, but beside him, blocking all hope of escape, is the Angry Nurse. And behind them both is the Scare Manager.

Everything stops.

The nice boy does his best to be nonexistent. He tries so hard not to exist that you can hear the pathetic melting sound of him trying to turn himself into a tiny mop puddle so that he might trickle sideways out of the room and down the corridor to disappear, forever.

My son looks astonished, the way he does.

The Angry Nurse smiles.

Then the Scare Manager, with his expensive gold risk-watch and his bedside manners, fills the whole room with those words of his. Words that don't connect to things, or even to other words, but only make him bigger and his gold watch golder. More golden.

Words like Final. Like Contravention. Like Probationary. Like Terminate. Or possibly Exterminate, because the Angry Nurse's smile expands, and the nice boy makes no sound at all as the last few droplets of him . . . evaporate.

But the Scare Manager has even more words. Process. Professionalism. Team, which is never good. Before he can say Holistic, or Person-Centered, I leave my window and come to the rescue.

"We were just playing Scrabble," I say.

But it's too late. There is nothing of the nice boy left.

The Angry Nurse smiles.

So does the Scare Manager, but there is nothing about how good I look, none of his little jokes about how the fellows on my floor better watch out. He does, however, call me Rose.

"Rose," he says. "It appears that the time has come for a Comprehensive Review of your Individual Care Plan."

"My Invidious Scare Plan?" I say, but my heart isn't in it.

"Necessary. Adjustments. Change. Of. Location. Issues. Personal Safety. Security. Enhancement of. Risk. Minimization of. Patient Management. Achieving Best Practice Benchmarks in. Going forward."

My son looks around the room the way he does. But this time differently.

Something is about to be taken from me.

Not my room, please.

Not that. Not my room. Not that. Because not my window. Not my window, please. Not that. Not my window. Please.

I have not looked at whatever it is the nice boy wrote in the diary. I have needed to be with the older fellow in the garden.

We sit side by side on a bench in the sunshine, holding hands, with flowers all around us. Gardenia. Chrysanthemum. Azalea. Rhododendron. Forget-me-not. And all around us also, the birds make their noise.

"We must never forget this," I say.

"We will forget everything," he says. "One day," he says. "That's what happens," he says.

That can't be right.

"I will never forget," I tell him.

He doesn't say anything.

"I won't ever forget that I love you," I say.

"Of course you won't," he says. He doesn't say anything else.

Then he squeezes my hand.

The noise of the birds is deafening.

But there is danger. There is the Comprehensive Review of my Scare Plan.

So I go to the big diary to see what the nice boy has written, because I need all the help I can get.

It isn't easy to find it. Things that I expect to be in the diary are not necessarily there. Other things come as something of a surprise.

I wonder if more pages have been removed. More secret pages, secretly removed.

I must concentrate.

The nice boy has hidden his message very cleverly. He is very good at hiding things.

What he has written is barely there. Almost nonexistent.

Yet there it is.

It certainly isn't much. His handwriting is very beautiful, but there isn't much of it.

It is just four letters.

Getf.

That's it. That's all.

Not even finished.

Get f. Unfinished.

Get fucked.

I have to admit that it is something of a disappointment.

At least it sounds like him. Looks like, sounds like. Is . . . characteristic of him.

I read it again.

And again.

I keep reading it.

Until it begins to look different.

And yet it is the same way he says everything he says, the same way he does everything he does. Not entirely complete. Not completely entire. Not entirely one thing or another.

But he did come into my room. He certainly did do that, if not certainly. He certainly came into my room, uncertainly, and went all the way over to the big diary. And picked up the pen. And began to write. So why didn't he finish? Why did he stop? Why did he give up?

Or did he? Or did he . . . alleviate . . . ameliorate? Abbreviate.

It's what he does, the nice boy. Abbreviates. Cuts off his beautiful fringe, swallows half of what he says, spits out the rest. Wonders around without his mop.

It is the same way he does everything he does. Does it and doesn't do it. Speaks and stays silent. Stays silent, and yet tells me things.

Not exactly forward, not entirely backward.

More or less sideways.

Get f.

Or *F get?*

It makes me think of Charity and Felicity and the things they say about the nice boy. The things they seem so certain of about the nice boy, about whom everything seems so uncertain.

Trans, they say. Didge, they say. Short for Indigenous, they say. Short for. Abbreviation of. Aspy, they say. Short for Asperger's, they say. Inter, they say. Short for intersex. I think they make some of this stuff up. But they seem so certain. Lexy, they say. Means he's dyslexic, Granma, they say. Means he gets everything back to front, they say.

Or sideways.

Get f.

Or *F get.*

Get fucked, or *Fucked get?*

F get.

Or *forget?*

Forget.

That's what the nice boy has written. Has tried to write. Has tried to write and at the same time tried not to write.

Forget.

What does it mean? Why is it important?

What is he trying to tell me? What does he know?

I have no idea.

Perhaps I have forgotten.

But I do remember the danger. I do remember the threat. I do remember the Comprehensive Review of my Scare Plan.

Change.

Location.

My room. My window.

And through my window, beyond my window, the garden.

And in that garden, the older fellow and the love.

Not the garden. Not that, please. Please, not that.

My son. My daughter. I need their help. It occurs to me that per-haps I will even ask them for it. Help me, my son. Help me, my daughter, please. Please, help me.

What nonsense. They already help me. They are always helping me. They write in the big diary, they carry potted plants to the bathtub.

But they are also babies: babies in an old photograph having their toes tickled by a man with no head.

And the nice boy says forget.

Yet surely I need to remember. I need to remember. Shirley. Remember what?

I look at the picture of my headless husband, tickling the toes of my children.

There is love in that picture.

There is even happiness.

I wonder how it got there.

You can see love in the way he tickles those toes. You can see happiness in the children. In their tiny, happy toes.

My son. My daughter. My happy daughter. My happy son.

No, that doesn't sound like them at all.

Perhaps I have not paid sufficient attention to their toes.

Love.

Happiness.

Yet there is no happiness in the tear along the top of the photograph, no love in the torn jagged edge across the top of my headless husband's neck, that neck with its nasty lines.

There is anger.

There is fear.

Fear?

Who is afraid?

I am, of course.

There is fear, certainly, in that ragged tear across the top of the picture, as well as anger and nastiness. But it doesn't quite seem to . . . what do you call it? It seems to not quite . . . attach. Adhere. Add here.

I need not to play games with words. Need to not play games with words.

I need to remember.

And to remember the need.

I remember those lines on his neck because they stood out, like his neck, against his always white collar and above his usual blue tie. Above. Against. Always. Usual.

He always liked to wear a collar and tie. Now, who likes to wear a collar and tie? Who, now, likes to wear a collar and tie? Nobody, that's who. Although I can't be certain, obviously. But my first husband was not nobody. I am certain of that. And I don't think he wore a collar and tie only because he had to, as part of his . . . what do you call it? Profession.

His profession. He had one, I'm sure.

Bank teller? Who can tell? Financial adviser? Hedgehog fund manager?

Cabinet minister? Furniture salesman?

Accountant? White ant? Pissant?

CEO? VIP? POTUS? SCROTUM?

Or some other acrobat?

OMG, as Chastity and Felicity would say.

He was something, anyway.

Whatever, as Chastity and Felicity would also say.

But I am just being impossible. I remember what he was. It is very boring to remember it, but I do remember.

He had investments. He managed them.

He was infested with investments.

His investments were very successful.

And he had invested in me. I was to be managed.

So, most of his investments were successful. And could be managed.

He liked to wear a collar and tie, and the nasty lines on his neck stood out in contract . . . contempt . . . contrast against the stiff white collar and the blue tie tied tight. Tightly.

This I remember.

He had a way of extending that neck of his high above his collar and tie, lengthening, expanding, each lined segment rising up high above me.

Like a . . . concertina. An accordion. According to him.

Everything was according to him.

Accordingly, everything was about me looking up at that mighty expanding accordion of a neck.

"Look upon my mighty neck, which rises up so high above my collar and tie, and listen to what I say, accordionly."

And what he said was always about me, and what was wrong with me. Accordion to him.

He, so high above. And always right. Me, so far below. And always wrong.

It used to make me laugh. Not in a good way. Silently, secretly. Angrily.

And then, one day, off came his head.

I should speak to my children about this.

B ut first, there is the Comprehensive Review of my Scare Plan. This involves many clipboards, much questioning, the taking of my pulse and my temperature, the pressurizing of my blood, the tapping of my kneecap with tiny hammers, close inspection of my urine, and endless, awful smiling from the Angry Nurse.

My medication is reevaluated, reassessed, recalibrated, reclipboarded. The shapes and the colors of the pills and tablets change. The Bessarabian girl explains them all to me with great enthusiasm, as if they are delicious new treats from a magical candy shop. The Angry Nurse, being professional, refers to them as my new Therapeutic Intervention Regime.

My very own regime.

The Scare Manager is not directly involved in all this— at least, not in a hands-on, Person-Centered way. But I know he is in his office, being Holistic. I see my son there with him when my walker and I go wondering, and they have that look of two people talking about accounts and passwords.

"Just some routine restructuring," my son says when I ask him.

"Rooting and what?" I say.

He explains that there are some minor changes in the way my account does whatever it is that my account does.

"Miner changes? Like in the dark, underground, with a pick and whatsitsname? Shovel?"

He says it is a simple matter of reconfigured firewall settings and transactional protocols. I ask him if this is the same as the sign on the elevator warning me not to use it if I am on fire, regardless of whether I am under the influence of alcohol, transnational or otherwise.

"Mom," he says. "You can, of course, access your account at any time."

"Of course."

"Using your password," he says.

"My password," I say.

My daughter wants to talk about potted plants. I want to talk to her about love.

Kneeling by the bathtub, she tells me I have too many. Potted plants, not bathtubs.

I want to tell her I have too many headless first husbands. Too many Comprehensive Reviews of my Scare Plan.

Help me, my daughter, I want to say. I am afraid. Help me, please.

But of course she *is* helping me. She is putting my potted plants in the bathtub. But there are too many of them, she suggests. Everything about her suggests there are too many potted plants in her life.

I think about telling her that I don't care so much about the potted plants. I have the leaves and the trees in my window, and through the window, beyond the window, I have the garden with the older fellow.

But I don't tell my daughter this, because I think the potted plants are good for her. Because without them, without carrying them one by one from beneath the window and placing them carefully in the bathtub and watering them, and then returning them one by one to their place beneath the window, without all this, how would she be so busy and tired when she comes here, how would she serve and suffer, why would she rest her head on the edge of the bathtub as if she can't go on?

And also because I have a suspicion. I suspect. Not a good thing, I know, to suspect my daughter, who helps me and is so busy and tired and believes in God and has Felicity and Charity to worry about without worrying about her mother's potted plants. But I suspect that when my daughter is talking about potted plants and about how there are too many of them, what she really means is that I have too much room, too much room in my room. And that the next thing will be that I have too many windows, too many leaves and trees in my window, too many gardens where I sit holding hands with older fellows while too many birds make too much noise about love. What she really means is that I have too much.

What she really means is the Comprehensive Review of my Scare Plan.

Change. Of. Location.

This suspicion, which I shouldn't have, reminds me of her brother and the way he looks around the room when he tells me about changes to my account, routine reconfigurations and miners changing things in the dark, even though I can access the new transactional protocols simply by using my password, of course, any time I like. Even though it is not a good thing to suspect my son, who is such a good son and wipes his bottom so thoroughly.

When I hear my son and my daughter say these things it sounds like I am hearing the Scare Manager, and it makes me wander.

The fellow who doesn't live here said everything is changed. His account. His room. Everything.

So I am suspicious, and I am afraid. And I need to talk to my daughter about love. I need to ask her about the photo of her and her brother and their headless father.

"You look happy in this picture," I say. "Were you happy? That doesn't seem like you."

She rests her head on the side of the bathtub.

"They are definitely your toes. And your brother's."

She sighs. She is so very tired.

"And love. There is love. How did it get there? Where did it come from? Where did it go?"

It serves her right for telling me I have too many potted plants.

What is the correct number of potted plants? I wonder. Or the correct size of a room? Or the appropriate amount of love?

One thing is certain. That headless husband tickling the toes of my children knew what was correct, what was appropriate. He always did. Even without his head, that neck with its nasty lines rising up above his collar and his tie, right up to the ragged line across the top of the picture where I tore off his head, that neck says it all. Despite the tickling of toes and the happiness and the love, what I see in his headless neck is exactly what I would see if his beheaded head was looking at me from over the happy heads of my children. I would see what was correct. I would see what was not correct. What was not appropriate.

I am not correct. I am not appropriate. That is one thing, two things, I know for certain.

S ometimes I go on adventures in this place with my friend. She in her wheelchair, I with my walker. My friend moves more slowly than I do, being in a wheelchair. And being dead, obviously.

Nevertheless, my friend knows her way around even better than I do. I know my way around very well, but she seems to be aware of things that even I haven't noticed. This may be because she is dead, or mad, or because these things are not real, but nevertheless.

We begin simply enough, moving along the corridors. I hope at these times that we don't come across the nice boy who mops the floors. It seems that I do not wish to share the nice boy with anyone. Or perhaps I am a little ashamed of my friend. She could certainly present herself better, it's true. Always she wears that meatball-stained nightgown with the blue whatsitsnames around the collar. Whereas I, of course, take the trouble to wear a nice blouse. I care about my appearance. As the nice boy does also, in his way.

But the nice boy is nowhere to be seen, and we move through the corridors and my friend encourages me to notice the other poor souls in this place, whom as a rule I am not all that interested in. In whom, as a rule, I am not all that interested.

But my friend is curious, if also cruel.

"Will you take a look at that," she'll say, pointing at some sad bugger sitting against the wall dribbling or shuffling along being cheerful. Or we will look in at a room where the door is open, or if the door is closed she'll just open it and we'll look in anyway, because who's going to stop us? Anyway, what's to see? They'll be in there lying in bed with their mouth open, or sitting in the chair beside their bed with their mouth open, and high up in a corner the TV will be on, showing people sitting behind a table agreeing with each other, or eating hamburgers with extreme happiness, or driving cars much too fast through rivers.

Sometimes my friend tells me stories about the people in these rooms.

"This is Mrs. Zbtosmty," she might say. "She is a vampire, you know."

Or else she might pretend to have a conversation. She is much more sociable than I am. She talks to anyone, smiling at them and being extremely unpleasant. Naturally they think that she wants to be their friend, and they will try to tell her about their lives. She will pretend to listen to them, and when they have finished she will roll her eyeballs and say, "Blah blah blah blah blah blah."

My friend even speaks other languages. We might meet, just as an example, a Chinese person or a New Zealander, and after we have stood there for a while listening to them gabbling on about their lives, my friend will say, "Blah blah blah blah blah blah," in a perfect Chinese or New Zealand accent.

There is a room she takes me to, and she opens the door and there are three people in there, lying in three different beds. All their mouths are open. At first I think they must be dead, except that the TV is on. Certainly they don't look like they are about to do anything any time soon.

"Don't let them fool you," my friend tells me. "They fuck

all night long. Sometimes I get no sleep at all because of their fucking."

"Really?" I say.

"All night long," she says. "Fucking, fucking, fucking. Sometimes I have to come and bang on the door and yell at them to stop all that fucking, but they just ignore me and keep on fucking, all night long."

"Really?" I say. "All night long?"

"All night long," she says. "Fuck, fuck, fuck."

My friend is enjoying this. I'm quite enjoying it myself.

Nevertheless, we must continue our adventures. We use the revelator to go down to the next level. First, of course, we have a laugh about the sign that tells us not to use it if we happen to be on fire. Second, while we wait for the doors to open, my friend tells me I should be aware of the Fiery Escape stairs. I tell her that of course I am perfectly well aware of the Fiery Escape stairs, because there they are right beside the revelator and I see them there every time I go down to the next level. I could even take those stairs to get there if I chose, which is more than can be said for my friend, on account of her being in a wheelchair, not to mention dead.

Nevertheless, she insists that we open the Fiery Escape door and take a look down those stairs. Which is not easy, neither the opening nor the looking, since the whatsitsname is broken and the fire that the stairs lead to must be so far below that it doesn't cast any glow.

"Look," my friend says.

"I'm looking," I tell her.

"Don't forget," she says.

I am becoming a little tired of people telling me that.

"Don't forget," she continues, "that they could throw you down these stairs and break your neck any time they like."

This isn't funny, but it makes me laugh. As if she and I aren't aware that there would be no need for them to go to all that trouble when they could just push me out of my own window. Any time they like.

Nevertheless, she seems satisfied at having given me this warning, so we get into the revelator and descend together to the lower levels.

Here I begin to understand how much my friend has come to know. It isn't that the things I see are unfamiliar, but she encourages me to see them in a different way. Down here, along the corridor that leads toward the big main entrance doors, there is the beauty parlor, where you can get a pedophile or have your hair dyed blue, and the media room, where you can go to sleep in front of enormous, deafening feel-good films in enormous, comfortable chairs with holders on the side for a cup, or your teeth. And there is the IT lounge, which has two computers, one of which is broken, and in one corner a pile of old *Encyclo*-whatsitsname *Britannica*s, which are tattered and smelly, although unbroken.

My friend seems to think I know nothing about these facsimiles. Facilities.

"I have found this very useful for doing my research," she says with great self-importance, waving vaguely toward the computers so that I can't even be sure whether she means the unbroken one.

"I do most of my research on my smart phone," I lie. "With my thumbs."

But she is already telling me something else. About either the beauty parlor or the media room, I forget which.

"Here I have personally witnessed," she tells me, almost whispering for the evil excitement of it.

"Personally?" I say, just to slow her down and increase the excitement for both of us.

"I have personally witnessed some poor bugger having a plastic bag put over their head."

"Plastic?" I say, but she will not be interrupted.

"Tied at the bottom so they couldn't breed. Breathe."

This is surprising, I suppose. My friend certainly wants me to be surprised. But, somehow, it doesn't surprise me at all. Not as much as the fucking, anyway.

"And later, no doubt, thrown down the stairs into the fire."

Speaking of down, we then descend farther, to a level I don't believe I have ever visited before. My friend is determined to surprise me now.

"Somewhere down here," she tells me, "is the secret place." As if she is not quite so certain of her facts, but even more excited. "This is where the drugs are bought and sold. And the pieces."

"Pieces, like silk?"

"Pizzas, like food. To entice the little children. The poor little kiddies that they bring in here to drain the blood from, for their unspeakable rites."

I ask her who *they* are, these ones with the unspeakable rights, but the impression I get is that my friend is not entirely sure, although she is reasonably confident that they include politicians and archbishops and possibly lizard people.

Finally, somehow, we find ourselves near the main entrance, standing outside the closed door of the Scare Manager's office, and it is here that I begin to wonder whether my friend's knowledge is, in fact, all that reliable. Because she tells me, pointing and whispering, that this is the laundry.

"Where it all gets laundered," she says.

What rot. I have seen the laundry. It's all trolleys piled high with big bags filled with towels and sheets that get taken away by trucks and then returned with all the life boiled out of them until they are shiny and thin and almost gray, like meatballs.

But my friend is incessant. Insistent. This, she assures me, putting her ear to the locked door where it says "Scare Manager," is where the laundering happens.

She sees my septic look.

"Once," she tells me, "I came down here and found it unlocked. In the middle of the night, with my flashlight, when I had been kept awake by all that fucking. And I saw it."

"The fucking?"

"The laundering."

She is very proud of herself.

I learn so much during these adventures with my friend. It's really quite exhausting. Not that I ever remember any of it afterward.

Nevertheless.

T he nice boy wrote *forget*. But I want to remember.

Not my headless first husband.

Not even my nighttime adventures with my friend.

What I want to remember is the older fellow.

So that's what I do.

I am in the garden in the sunshine with the older fellow with the lovely spots on his neck, and we are surrounded by flowers and birds and love. *Gardenia magnifica*.

"Lettuce," he says.

"Let us what?" I say.

He laughs.

"No," he says. "Lettuce. We should plant some."

"Cos?" I ask.

"Cos we both like eating it, and we don't have any right now in the vegetable patch," he says, and I laugh, then he laughs again. Perhaps the birds laugh too. They certainly make a noise.

This kind of silliness is something we do. It is not something that the other fellow, the headless fellow with the nasty neck, would ever have done. Silliness, and laughter, were not what a fellow like that with a neck like that in a collar and tie like that would ever . . . entertain. Allow. Entertainment Allowance. I had to entertain myself, and even though his neck in that collar and tie seemed to me to be silly, if not entertaining, I was not allowed to laugh.

I try something with my son and my daughter. The next time they visit, I tell them I have been thinking about windows.

"I have been thinking about windows," I say. "About windows, and about windowsills. I have been thinking a great deal about the whole subject of window silliness."

When I say this to my son, he just looks around the room.

When I say it to my daughter, she puts her forehead down on the edge of the bathtub and sighs.

They are both so much like their father.

The fellow who doesn't live here looks down at his plate. It's not meatballs today. It's fish fingers. They don't look like fish. They don't even look like fingers.

I look up at the smiling sharks, balancing their beach balls on the wall. At the smiling sharks on the wall, balancing their beach balls.

"They have changed my room again," he says to the fish fingers.

I am sorry I asked him my usual question about which floor he is on. It only seems to cause him pain. Apparently, I do not wish to cause him pain.

"And my account," he says.

"Your account?" I say.

It seems so long ago that he didn't live here and wasn't so sad about everything.

"It is all changed," he says.

"Changed?" I say. Change. I am so tired of that word.

He looks at his fish fingers as if they, at least, won't change. They never change, any more than the meatballs.

"My account. My password. Everything is changed. Things are moved about. Amounts differ. Money disappears. Nothing is the same. Passwords. Log-ins."

"Log inns?"

"Security codes. Transactional protocols."

"Transnational alcohols?" I say. I hope he might laugh.

He doesn't laugh. Looking at him is like looking into a plate of fish fingers. I touch his hand. In no way is it like holding the hand of the older fellow in the garden.

"How about your medication?" I ask him.

"All changed," he says, and he begins to cry.

"Stop that," I say. It's disgusting.

"There has been a Comprehensive Review of my Care Plan," he says.

OMG, as Felicity and Chastity would say.

And now they have changed *my* room.

I return from my wondering, and there it is. A piece of silk hangs from the door handle. The silk, and the door handle, look so . . . what do you call it? Inoculated. Innocuous.

I manage to get my walker through the doorway.

The Phoenician girl is in there, with a cardboard box. She takes pictures out of the box and does her best to fit them all on the whatsitsname. I recognize the pictures. The Dresser family. And there is the big diary. It looks bigger than ever.

A TV is on the wall. It is a large TV, a small wall.

There is a window. Below the window there are a certain number of potted plants.

Beside the window, there is a wheelchair.

In the window, through the window, there is a parking lot.

I go looking for a room without a piece of silk on the door handle. And there it is.

And there is my window, with the leaves and the trees.

And there, in my bed, is the fellow with the nasty lines on his neck. And his mouth open. And his pajamas.

He can afford to be here, it seems.

The TV is on. On the TV an archbishop, or a child molester, is leaving a building and is helped into a car. Probably he is being taken on an outing, to somewhere nice for morning tea. The nasty fellow watches this on the TV. At least, his eyes are open and they are turned toward the TV. His eyes and his mouth, and his pajamas.

The Carthaginian girl comes in and catches me trying to push the nasty fellow out of the bed.

"Be nice," she says.

"Be nice? Look at the nasty lines on this fellow's neck."

It's no use. Behind her is the Angry Nurse.

"Come along, dear," the Angry Nurse says. "Back to your room."

And she smiles.

"How are you finding your room?" my son asks.

"Easy," I say. "It's the one without a piece of silk on the door handle."

He looks around the room, which doesn't take him very long.

"What is that wheelchair doing there?" I ask. Although of course it isn't doing anything. Just standing there. Sitting there. As if it is looking out the window. At the parking lot.

"You're legible for it," I think he says. Then he tells me it is part of my new Individual Person-Centered Scare Package, consistent with revised Safety Guidelines and Best Practice Security Alcohols. It is easy to see who he's been talking to. To whom he's been talking.

"And what am I supposed to do with it?" I say. "Exactly?"

I am supposed to use it instead of my walker. I am supposed to sit in it, instead of wondering the way I do. I am supposed to use it to go to the dining room, where I am supposed to sit in it and stare at my Person-Centered mashed potato.

I ask my daughter the same question. She sighs. Her life is so busy, she doesn't have time to answer questions about wheelchairs. There are fewer potted plants, though this doesn't mean she has more time. Felicity and Charity are busy preparing for their final examinations. They are standing by the window with their smart phones, and you can tell how busy they are by their thumbs.

Felicity, or Charity, sits in the wheelchair to show me how fun it is.

"How fun is this, Granma?" she says, her thumbs not stopping for a second.

"Be careful, Felicity," I say.

"Charity," says my daughter, and sighs.

"Whatever," says Charity.

"You might fall out the window," I say.

Felicity and Charity laugh, their thumbs still moving.

"It's happened before," I say.

My daughter sighs.

I try it. I sit in the wheelchair. I don't wish to be difficult. But I don't wheel it anywhere. Not wheely. Ha-ha. That must be the

new medication. I use it as a chair. I sit in it and look out the
window.

At the parking lot.

There are lines painted on it, for parking spaces. A car arrives, parks between the lines, then leaves with someone in the
passenger seat and their wheelchair folded up in the what do you
call it . . . trunk, to go somewhere nice for morning tea. Somewhere wheely, wheely nice.

I must stop doing that.

It's not much of a window.

My window was better.

This was my friend's window, and it was never as good as my
window.

My friend, who I used to play Scrabble with. With whom I
used to play Scrabble.

I used my friend to play Scrabble with.

She cheated, anyway.

And then one day she was delivered in the parking lot. On
her back in her nightgown with blue forget-me-nots at the
neck.

Myosotis scorpioides.

I haven't forgotten.

I haven't forgotten anything.

Or at least not everything.

I sit in the wheelchair by the window. It is, they remind me, *my*
wheelchair. It is not, I remind them, *my* window.

They. Them.

The Minoan girl. The Angry Nurse. The Scare Manager.

The Minoan girl gives me a cup of tea and my new medication, then leaves the room.

Which leaves the Scare Manager looking at me, with the parking lot behind him. And behind me, with her hand on the back of

my wheelchair, is the Angry Nurse. I can't see her, but I know she is smiling.

I think they mean to kill me.

The Scare Manager tells me it is impossible.

Not killing me; that is possible. That is very possible. The Angry Nurse could kill me with one good push.

What is not possible is me. I am impossible. I am a situation, and it is an impossible one. It is an Impossible Situation, the Scare Manager says. I cannot be wondering about, going to other people's rooms and attaching bits of silk to their door handles, or dragging them out of their beds when they are watching TV in their pajamas with their mouths open, and then looking out their windows.

"It is a Health and Safety issue," the Scare Manager tells me. "A Duty of Care issue."

"Duty of Care issue," I hear the Angry Nurse say behind me. She says it to remind me she is there and could kill me at any moment.

"A Risk Minimization issue," the Scare Manager says, because he doesn't like the Angry Nurse to have the last word. We have something in common, he and I. I want to turn myself around to face the Angry Nurse and ask her not to stand behind me where I can't see her smiling, but I won't give her the satisfaction. And I can't move this damned wheelchair.

What this is, I want to tell them, is a window issue. A changing-my-window-so-that-I-lose-my-beautiful-garden issue. A forgetting issue and a remembering issue. Not to mention a selling-people's-rooms-to-other-people-who-can-afford-to-pay-more issue.

And yet I don't tell them this, because I know that if I say the wrong thing the Angry Nurse will tip the wheelchair forward and I will slip so easily out of the open window and I will be in that parking lot. On my back in that parking lot with my head broken, staring at the sky. Just like my friend. With or without a nightgown, with or without any forget-me-nots around the neck.

Without, actually. Because I am properly dressed, as always.

When they murder me, when they push me out this window and
I am on my back in the parking lot with my head broken staring
at the sky, I will be wearing a nice pantsuit. Pant suit. Pants suit. I
like to look my best.

The Scare Manager looks his best too, I'll give him that. He
makes an effort. If he murders me, at least we will both look the
part.

He looks quite handsome, in fact. I don't think it's just the
new medication. Although I can't be sure, obviously.

As well as his expensive gold watch, he wears a shiny new
leather jacket. And pants, of course. Not leather pants, but
pants. He would not murder me with no pants on. Would not,
with no pants on, murder me. That would be unprofessional.
That would not be Best Practice. That would not meet Benchmarks.

He dresses differently now. Not at all like a doctor, or whatever he was. His clothes look expensive. Like his new gold risk-
watch, like his new gold car. Beneath his new leather jacket he
wears a yellow, or perhaps it is gold, whatsitsname. Tortoise shell.
Turtle neck. Turtleneck.

What is it about necks?

Fellows and their necks.

"Rose," he says, the way people do when they want me to understand things, "you need to understand."

Then he talks about Duty of Care again, then Best Practice.
Then he says Person-Centered, then Reevaluation of Scare Pa-
rameters Going Forward. Then Facilitating a Holistic Thera-
peutic Environment, then Problematic Behavioral issues, not to
mention Balancing Person-Centered Scare Needs with Broader
Management Priorities through Continuous Assessment and
Review of Flexible Response Hexameters and Addressing of
Key Security Concerns through Ongoing Adjustment of Indi-
vidual Mobility Regimes and Reconfigured Administrative and
Financial Pathways.

"It's important to us that you understand, Rose," he says, as if

I am a lovely, brainless old thing instead of just an impossible one. "Or else we could just tip this wheelchair forward and watch you slide right out this window and end up dead in that parking lot in your pantsuit."

Or else it's the medication.

"What about my account?" I say.

Behind me, the Angry Nurse smiles and grips the back of my wheelchair more tightly.

In front of me, the Scare Manager smiles too. It is not as bad as the smile of the Angry Nurse, but it is bad enough.

"Rose," he says. "You don't need to worry yourself about that, Rose."

Rose. Rose. Rose. The way they use my name.

It makes me remember my headless first husband. Whenever he used my name, his neck would expand and he'd look down at me from its mighty height.

"Rose!" he'd say.

Or he'd say, "Rose?" Or, "Really, Rose?" Or, "Rose, really!"

Or did he?

I remember him using my name. I even remember the puncture marks. Punctuation marks. I'm just not sure I remember *Rose*.

Did he use some other name?

Whatever, as Felicity would say. Or Chastity.

Whatever name he called me, whenever I heard it, it always meant the same thing.

It meant that he disapproved. Disassociated himself from. Was disappointed by. Disdainful of. Disgusted at.

Then his head, disassociated from his neck, disappeared. As if I had made it happen.

I wonder if I could make the Scare Manager disappear? His head, anyway. If he was a photograph, I would certainly cut off his head, right above that golden turtle of his.

I would do it Holistically, of course. It would be Person-Centered. It would certainly be Best Practice, going forward.

Which makes me remember when I went to my room, the one with no piece of silk on the door handle and no parking lot in the window, and there in my bed was the other fellow with his mouth open, and his pajamas.

I remember pushing him out of the bed. It wasn't easy. I remember trying to drag him across the floor to the window. That was even uneasier. More difficult. Then I remember deciding not to push him out the window. I don't remember why. Oh yes, it was because I didn't want him to be lying there in my garden with his neck broken. All I wanted in that garden was the older fellow and the flowers and the birds and the love.

So, if I remember rightly, and right now I think I do, I tried to drag the nasty fellow into the bathroom, with the idea of putting him in the bathtub.

But I gave up; it was too difficult. Although it was fun trying.

It was fun imagining my daughter coming to water my potted plants and finding him in the bathtub. She might have thought he was God. Since God seems to be in there with her whenever she kneels with her forehead on the edge of the tub and sighs and seems to be saying some sort of prayer.

What would she do if she found God in my bathtub? Play with his toes?

Because thinking all this also makes me remember the photograph of my headless first husband playing with the toes of my daughter and my son. As if he is God, and has the divine right to tickle the toes of my children.

While I'm remembering all these things, I'm forgetting other things. Like what it was that I was saying to the Scare Manager standing in front of me with his golden turtle, while behind me the Angry Nurse smiles and prepares to push me out the window.

Then I remember, or else it's the medication.

"I need to talk about my account," I say.

"Rose . . ." the Scare Manager begins to say.

"Something is going on with my account," I say.

Something seems to happen behind the Scare Manager's turtle.

"Something strange," I say. "Something illegible. Illegal."

And behind me, something seems to happen to the Angry Nurse. I feel her smile. Differently.

"I know all about it," I say.

M y son and I are going to talk about my account.
It says so right there in the big diary.

I know what is happening with my account. I know all about it.
That is what it says in the diary. It isn't true, but that's what it says.

I know because I wrote it, on the page that says tomorrow.

It is an experiment.

I wait for my son to arrive and see what the diary says. While I wait, I do another experiment. I perform another experiment. Like a performer. I undertake another experiment. Like an undertaker. Anyway, it's an experiment.

I sit in the wheelchair, in the window, and I hold the photo of the older fellow in my lap. In my lap, I hold the photo of the older fellow. I look at the photo. I look out the window. I look at the photo again. Then I look out the window. It doesn't work. It is still a parking lot. No garden. Straight lines. Arrows. This way, that way. Little square hedges like tight boxes. No, not square.

Rectangular. Rectilinear. Rectal. The parking lot is not unlike a thoroughly wiped bottom.

And now here is my son, driving into the parking lot, following the arrows, parking inside the lines. He is a good son. Perhaps he is here to take me somewhere nice for morning tea. Since he hasn't seen the diary and doesn't know that we are going to talk about my account.

And, oh dear. Here is the Scare Manager running out into the parking lot to catch my son before he can even get out of his car. As if he has been waiting in his office by the big sliding entrance doors and as soon as he has seen my son arrive in the parking lot he has leaped up in his leather jacket and his gold turtleneck and punched in the secret code on the little Scrabble board thing, unless he doesn't even need to because the big doors open by themselves just because he wants them to.

Anyway, there he suddenly is beside my son's car, talking at my son through the car window before my son can get himself out, and he is not happy at all. I can't hear what he says to my son, obviously, but he is obviously not making any of his little jokes. When I think of it, which I do now, he doesn't make his little jokes at all anymore. They were bad jokes, but nevertheless. For all his gold watches and gold cars and solid gold turtles, he is not a happy Scare Manager.

I watch him, through my window, being very unhappy through the window of my son's car, waving his arms about in his leather jacket so the sunlight glints off his risk-watch and his golden turtle, and when my son finally manages to get out of his car, he is a very unhappy-looking son. I don't like that, obviously. I don't want my son to be an unhappy son.

But things are happening, at least. And that's fun. How fun is this, Granma? as Felicity and Charity sometimes ask. Rectangularly. Rhetorically. Things are happening, all right. Maybe things are even changing. And change is good, obviously. Although it doesn't look like it right now in that parking lot.

When my son is finally able to get out of his car and walk

toward the entrance, the Scare Manager still doesn't stop talking at him. My son has his head down as if he is searching for flowers in the parking lot, flowers that aren't there. And his head is nodding, as if he knows there are no flowers in the parking lot and accepts that there never could be flowers in such a parking lot. And the Scare Manager still won't stop talking at him.

I move away from the window to the big diary that says my son is coming to talk to me about my account.

But then the Angry Nurse comes in with her clipboard and pressurizes my blood and bangs my knee with her tiny hammer. Perhaps her plan is to kill me before my son arrives. Not with the tiny hammer, obviously, although if anyone could kill someone with such a hammer, it would be the Angry Nurse.

She writes something on her clipboard.

"My son is coming to speak to me about my account," I tell her, just in case she does intend to kill me. She doesn't need a hammer. She could kill me with that clipboard.

She looks at me.

"He is on his way," I tell her, playing for time. "He'll be here any minute."

"You must not forget," she says.

I wish people would make up their minds. Forget. Don't forget.

"You need to remember," she says.

"It's written right here in the diary," I tell her.

"You need to remember," she says. "That we are here to help you."

And then she smiles, so I know I really am in danger.

Before she can smile again, my son arrives. He has the look of someone who has been hit many times with many tiny hammers.

"Here he is now," I say. She can't kill us both, surely.

"Mom," he says, and looks around the room.

"Son," I say, and I pretend to read what it says in the big diary. "You are here to talk about my account, I believe."

Once the Angry Nurse leaves, we do indeed talk about my account, though not before I ask if he had any trouble finding my room.

"But of course, you would know it by the piece of silk on the door handle," I say, and he looks like I've just hit him with another little hammer.

"Mom," he says, "do you have any worries about your account?"

"Worries?" I say. "Account?"

There is a parking lot in my window. Why should I make it easy for him?

He looks around the room the way he does, and I do feel a certain amount of pity for him. He is a good son, and wipes his bottom thoroughly.

"I have been taking a close look at my account," I lie, to get things started.

"You do trust me, don't you, Mom?" he says.

"You're a good son," I say. I don't say anything about his bottom.

"I understand what's going on," I say, which is such a lie I almost laugh.

Talk about getting things started. My son begins to talk about my account. He speaks with his head down, not looking at me or even at the room, though sometimes he actually looks out the window as if he's searching for flowers in the parking lot, nodding to himself as if he's still listening to the unhappy Scare Manager talking at him, still being hit with all those hammers.

My son talks about change, and eternity. He talks about minor adjustments which have had to be made, and he reminds me that he has the Power of Eternal.

"Mom, there have been certain cash flow issues I've had to deal with."

"Cash flow issues?"

"Temporary hiccups in the investment market . . ."

Why wouldn't I feel sorry for him? Who would want their own son to have issues with flowing and hiccuping?

"I get temporary hiccups," I tell him, trying to help. "I think it's the meatballs. Or the fish fingers."

"You do trust me, Mom," he says. "Don't you, Mom?"

He talks about the need to be flexible, and my own good, and the Power of Eternal again, and about how he has been working closely with Scare Management to ensure that monies are available as necessary to respond to necessary adjustments in my Scare Plan. Listening to him is like hearing the tap-tap-tapping of hundreds of tiny hammers.

My son is a good son, and he is lying to me about money.

But the thing is, I don't really care about money. What am I going to spend it on? Bingo? Meatballs?

What I care about is my room. Well, not my room. It's just a room. My window. That's what I care about. And in my window, through my window, whether there is a parking lot or whether there is a garden. And, if there is a garden, whether there are flowers and birds and an older fellow and . . . everything.

"Some things will never change," my son says. I suppose he is talking about the Power of Eternal.

"Some things never change," I agree. "Meatballs, for example. And some things appear to change very quickly."

He looks out the window. Then he talks to me about my needs. How I need to cooperate with Scare Management, how I need to comply with the changing requirements of my Scare Plan, how I need to not challenge every little change, how change is good and how I need to think of it as a challenge.

Change. No change. Challenge. Don't challenge. My son has a perfectly normal neck, but right now I feel like I am hearing his father, my headless husband. And I wish I was hearing the nice boy who mops the floors. Or even the fellow who doesn't live here. Or, of course, the older fellow in the garden.

I want to talk to my son about my friend who ended up on her back in the parking lot staring up at the sky. And about the fellow in my friend's bed who is now in my bed, and the nasty lines on his neck, and how I know he is there because he can afford to pay.

But I decide not to talk to my son about these things. My son is a good son, and he is busy enough right now, lying to me about money.

"Mom," he says, "you know your password. . . ."

"My password?" I say. "Of course I know my password. Everybody knows my password."

"No, Mom. Only *you* know your password. And me, of course, because I have the Power of Eternal. But any time you want to look at your account, you can. You know that, don't you?"

"Of course, and I'll know it is my account because it will have a bit of silk tied to it."

I wonder how he thinks I would look at my account, if I ever did, even if I did know my password. I have a phone beside my bed, but I am almost certain that it is not a smart one. And I certainly don't have thumbs like Felicity or Charity.

My son reads my mind.

"You do use the computers downstairs, don't you, Mom?"

"Of course I do," I say.

He means the IT lounge. The IT lounge that has two computers in it, one of which is broken. I know about computers, of course I do, I'm not completely what do you call it. I have even sat in front of those computers. I prefer the broken one. The one that isn't broken has a mountain on the TV part. It is an inspirational, snow-covered mountain such as you might see at the dentist. You can sit in front of this mountain for a long time and it never changes. Underneath it is a whatsitsname. Piano. Keyboard. It isn't like a Scrabble board, I am perfectly well aware of that. It is more like a typewriter, only modern. I have discovered that if you press any part of it, the snow-capped mountain disappears, which is certainly an improvement. But then a slot will appear, like a tiny letterbox, with a question in it that blinks at you. Winks at you. I do not know the answer to that question.

The only other thing in the IT lounge is the set of old whatsits dumped in one corner. Encirclements. Encyclicals. Encyclopedias. These ask you no questions, and provide useful and often quite fascinating information about Adirondacks and Marsupial and Xerxes. But nothing about my account.

"Anyway, you don't need to be worried, Mom," my son is telling me. "It isn't as if you need to understand every little thing."

"No," I agree. "Not every little thing."

"Some things are quite complicated, Mom."

"They certainly are, son."

He is a good son, but when he says this about every little thing, he reminds me again of his father, my headless husband. Don't you worry about that. Some things are too complicated. Just admire my collar and tie and my mighty neck, rising up like a mountain.

Then I think about people who are not like my first husband at all. Like the nice boy who mops the floors. Like the fellow who doesn't live here. Like the older fellow in the garden, with the lovely spots. People who try to let me know about things, instead of telling me I don't need to know them.

Now I feel afraid. I am afraid something has happened to the nice boy who mops the floors. I am afraid the fellow who doesn't live here is here no longer, or that if he is here, he is no longer the fellow who doesn't live here. I am afraid my son and the Scare Manager are attached to each other, tied to each other with lies and threats and golden turtles. I am afraid that the fellow with the nasty lines on his neck is in my bed because he can afford to pay more than I can, and that I have lost my window forever and that I will never see that garden again. Never again see that garden. I am afraid that the Angry Nurse will kill me and I will end up dead in the parking lot like my friend who cheated at Scrabble. I am afraid that I must remember, but what I must remember I don't entirely remember, and the nice boy told me that I must forget. Remember. Forget. Forget. Remember.

I am afraid that it may be my new medication.

And I am afraid that it may not be.

I undertake another experiment. With my walker and the photo of the older fellow and the piece of silk, I go to my room. My proper room, my real room, my previous room. Where the fellow with the nasty lines on his neck lies in my bed with his mouth open, and his pajamas. I tie the piece of silk to the door handle, to confuse the enemy. I should not think that way, obviously. Nevertheless.

There is no wheelchair by the window, because they do not intend to murder him, because he can afford to pay. Also because he never gets out of bed. My bed. Not that I am attached to the bed. I don't care about the bed. But the window. This window; my window.

I don't even bother to speak to him. He lies there, being able to afford to pay, with his mouth open above the nasty lines on his neck, and his nasty pajamas open, and the entire nastiness of him pointed toward the TV on the wall. He doesn't even know about the window. He is not attached to the window. He is attached to the bed. Ha-ha. He is attached to the bed by being able to afford to pay, by cash that flows and markets without hiccups.

I look at the window, and there is no parking lot. There are leaves. They do what leaves do. They leave. I look at the photo of the older fellow and I begin to feel that I am leaving too, that I leave and go through the leaves in the window and into the garden with the sunshine and the flowers and the older fellow beside me, and I begin to feel the older fellow's hand squeezing my hand, when the door opens and the Appalachian girl comes in with a piece of silk in her hand and tells me I must have been confused by this piece of silk being tied to the wrong door handle, and I tell her I was looking for bingo and agree that I have been led astray by mysteriously misplaced pieces of silk, and she offers to show me the way to bingo but on the way I say I've changed my mind because change is good and I must be flexible and so she takes me to my room instead, and she ties the piece of silk back onto the door handle and helps me into the wheelchair they have put there by the window, and when she leaves I look out that window and there is the fucking parking lot.

When my daughter comes to get the potted plants from beneath the window so she can put them in the bathtub, she stands there, confused. There are no potted plants.

"I threw them out the window," I tell her.

This is another experiment. What will my daughter do? I wonder.

What she does is she goes into the bathroom and begins to clean the bathtub. She kneels there and she scrubs that bathtub. She has never needed those potted plants, not really. Give her potted plants and she will water them. Give her a bathtub and she will scrub it. That's the way she is. God is with her in that bathroom.

I hate to interrupt the two of them, but out here by the window there is only myself, and Felicity and Chastity on their smart phones looking at graduation gowns. Felicity and Chastity both sit in the wheelchair while they do this, one on top of the other and fighting for space. They giggle and squirm and tickle each other, they tell each other to make room and to move over and to fuck off bitch, while all the time their thumbs are flying on those smart phones of theirs. Soon they will be at university. I move my walker to the doorway of the bathroom where my daughter kneels before God.

"I've been talking to your brother," I tell her. "He has been stealing from my account."

She sighs. But she doesn't put her head down on the edge of the bathtub the way she so often does. Instead, she looks at me.

"Mom," she says. "Everybody steals. Everybody cheats. Everybody lies."

This is progress.

"He is a good son," I say. "But there is something wrong about his cash flow, and he has hiccups and a temporary something or other in his investments."

Now she does put her head down on the edge of the bathtub, only for a moment. She is so tired. But she has her religion. She never quite stops scrubbing at a small dirty spot. I watch her as she forces herself to raise her head, to look at me again.

"He does his best, Mom," she says. "It isn't easy for him."

I have never been prouder of her. I have no idea what she is talking about, but nevertheless.

"And I was talking to him about you," I say.

"I'm sure that isn't true, Mom," she says.

"No, really, I was," I lie.

She is right, obviously. Everybody steals, everybody cheats, everybody lies.

Neither of them ever mentions the other. They have almost nothing in common. They have different lives. He has his business, his investments, his clean bottom. She has her busyness, her bathtubs, her Felicity and Charity. He has the Power of Eternal. She has God. Though they do have something in common, apart from me. They are, I suspect, the unhappiest people I have ever known. They may get that from their father, my headless first husband. And yet, in that photo, he tickles their toes and they are both giggling and looking up at the torn-off top of the photo where his head should be, and I suppose that if his head were there he might be giggling too, or at least laughing, although it is hard to imagine. Anyway, even with his head torn off there is actual happiness in that photo. Even love.

But there is a parking lot in my window instead of a garden, and another fellow is in my bed with his mouth open because he can afford to pay, and the Scare Manager drives a golden car and has a golden risk-watch and wears a golden turtle. Why should I be nice?

"Leave that bathtub alone," I tell her. "If you want to clean something, come here and do my toes."

Felicity and Chastity even look up from their smart phones for a second.

And my daughter does it, God bless her. She sits me down on the edge of the bed and takes off my shoes and washes my feet in warm water using the whatsitsname that lives under the bed in case of emergencies, and then she trims my toenails for me.

Felicity and Charity find this amazing, and tell me my toenails are revolting, and beg their mother to stop.

I am not at all surprised. She is a good daughter, and it is important for her to suffer.

It is nice having my toenails done. It puts me in the mood to chat.

"Your father is dead, right?"

She sighs. Which seems unfair. I am almost certain I have never asked her this question before.

"Poor Grandad," says Felicity. Or Chastity.

"I suppose it was his neck that killed him," I say.

"His . . . ?" my daughter says. Then she says, "A stroke. He died of a stroke, Mom. It was very sudden."

"How . . . what do you call it? Turgid. Tragic."

"Mom."

"Sorry."

I feel I should ask her more about her father. But I don't want to. I am an impossible cow.

It certainly has been good to talk, but I've lost interest in the subject, so while my daughter continues to suffer over my revolutionary toes, I ask Felicity and Charity if they have heard anything at school recently about the nice boy who mops the floors. I tell them he doesn't seem to work here anymore. Has he returned to school? Will he be going to the Graduation Ball?

"Ha-ha," says Felicity.

"As if," says Chastity.

He must have some friends at school, I suggest, who might know where he is, what he is doing. Friends who share his interests.

They seem to find this very funny indeed.

"Friends!" they say, as if the word is totally inexplicable . . . inapplicable.

"What about trans friends?" I say. "Inter friends? Didge friends? Aspy friends?"

They are impressed, I think, but only for a moment.

"Nofriends," says Felicity or Charity, saying it as if it is the nice boy's actual name, and for all I know it is. Niceboy No friends. They tell me they will see what they can find out, then they go back to their smart phones.

I don't want to think of him having no friends. Everyone has friends. Even I had a friend. Although she did cheat at Scrabble.

"The nice boy wrote in my diary," I tell them, but they don't hear me. They are busy with their thumbs and their graduation gowns. I imagine the nice boy at the Graduation Ball, wearing a beautiful graduation gown, cut to show off his new bosom.

"He has such lovely breasts," I recall, apparently aloud, because suddenly I have everyone's attention again.

"I think that will do, Mom," my daughter tells me, although it is possible that she is talking about my toes.

I am experimenting once more with the window, in the window, through the window, trying to get past the parking lot, through the parking lot, beyond the parking lot, and into the garden. It's not working. There is only the parking lot. There is no garden.

Then in comes the Angry Nurse. Through the door, not the window. She carries an armful of sorry-looking potted plants. She intends to kill me because she knows it was me who threw these miserable, unloved things out the window into the godforsaken parking lot.

I give her my best innocent look.

"Nice potted plants," I say.

They are bent and broken. Most of their leaves have left. There is barely any soil remaining in their pots.

She smiles and places the potted plants on the floor beneath the window. I wonder if she will kill me right away. Or will she make a speech first?

"Can I be of any help at all, dear?" she says.

It is to be the speech first, then.

"You must remember . . ." she begins, so I interrupt.

"I have never seen these potted plants before," I say.

The Angry Nurse says something about Safety.

"I wonder what these plants are called?" I say.

She says something about Well-Being, something about Duty of Scare.

"I don't know the names of any plants," I tell her. "I don't know anything about plants at all."

She smiles. She intends to kill me very soon.

"Don't forget, Rose, that we are here to help."

She will talk like this for a while. She will smile that smile of hers. She will get behind the wheelchair and then she will tip me out the window and I will die in the parking lot, looking at the sky.

The Angry Nurse and I understand each other.

I need to stop her from getting behind the wheelchair, so I ask her if she can help me by handing me one of the pictures from the whatsitsname.

She looks disappointed. She wants to kill me as quickly as possible, so she can get back to her office near the big sliding glass doors, so she can make plans with the Scare Manager for more cheating and lying and thieving and killing and laundering.

"Of course, dear," she says, and smiles. "Which picture would you like?"

I don't answer. I look at her as if I have already forgotten.

"You have so many lovely pictures," she says.

I see her fury, her savagery, I see how much she wants my blood, how much she wants this done.

So I wait for a while longer.

She smiles.

"They are pictures of my family," I say. "The Dresser family."

She can't help herself. She picks up a photo and hands it to me. She doesn't even look at it, doesn't even notice that it is torn across the top.

"Not that one," I tell her. "Why would I want to look at a photo with the top torn off? A picture of some headless fellow?"

She tries again.

"How about this one?" she says, smiling, thinking about my cracked skull on the parking lot concrete. "These are your grand-daughters, aren't they, Rose?"

Rose, indeed. I know what she's up to.

"Yes," I say. "That's Electricity, and that's Chutney. Or that one is Chutney, and that one is Electricity. Silly me. I'm not very good with names."

She looks at me. I wait until she smiles.

"They are about to . . . gravitate. Graduate."

"That's lovely, dear," she says.

I see the rage in her eyes.

"They go to school with the nice boy who mops the floors."

Her look is priceless, so I keep going. I tell her how I haven't seen the nice boy mopping the floors lately. Does she know what has happened to him? Will he be coming back soon?

This is not something she wishes to discuss.

"He is so nice," I say.

She says nothing.

"Don't you think?" I say.

She has to say something, so she turns back toward the pho-tos and mutters something about there being certain issues.

"Tissues?" I say.

"Behavioral issues," she says. "Not something for you to worry yourself about."

She then mutters something about Probationary. About Pending. About being stood down, subject to something.

"Subject," I repeat after her. "Object. Did the nice boy object?"

I'm almost certain I hear her sigh. I consider asking her if she would like to use my bathroom, so she can put her head down on the side of the bathtub the way my daughter does.

"Object," I say. "Objection. Obstruct. Obstruction. 'Do Not Obstruct.'"

Perhaps I've gone too far. She smiles at me as if I am very old and very, very stupid.

"Where is the photo of that headless fellow?" I say.

She hands it to me. Before she does, she briefly considers using it to stove in my skull. Stove. Stave. Steve. Words are so.

"These are my children," I tell her. "They are older now. Look at their toes."

She looks at their toes. She wants to kill me so badly, wants so badly to kill me, and instead she does what I tell her to do.

"They look so happy," the Angry Nurse says.

I almost laugh. What would she know about happiness? I wonder.

"And this is your husband?"

"Of course not," I tell her. "What would I be doing with a headless husband? This was my first husband. Later I got a better one. An older fellow."

She smiles. She knows I'm having trouble. She is quick to take advantage. She is good at what she does.

"What was his name, Rose?" she asks.

"Steve. Steven." I have no idea, and she sees it. "And of course, you know my children."

"Of course," she says, and I wait, but she doesn't say their names.

"Give me the photo of the older fellow," I tell her.

She pretends to have trouble finding it.

"It's there," I tell her. "Right there. In front."

She picks it up. She looks at it.

"Give it to me," I say. I am becoming tired of this game.

She holds it close, looks at it like it's a clipboard.

"Give it to me."

She gives it to me. She smiles.

"Your second husband?" she says.

I ignore the question. If she asks me his name, I will stand up and I will raise up the photo in its nice frame and I will steve in her skull with it. Stove. Stave.

She doesn't ask. She knows she is winning.

I hold it close. "Look at the lovely rosy spots on his neck," I say, because I know she can't see them.

And I think about how this photo used to be right at the back of the whatsitsname, behind all the others, and how every day, when my son came to visit, he would move this photo to the front. Never the one with himself and his sister and their happy toes and their headless father, but this one. What a good son. And what a good daughter, putting my potted plants in the bathtub every day even though she doesn't care about plants, doesn't even know their names.

Names. There are so many of them. They're like bits of silk attached to door handles. Maybe names are door handles, and things are attached to them, like bits of silk. Memories. Feelings. Whatever.

"What is his name?" the Angry Nurse says.

"He has no name."

She smiles. We understand each other.

"No name at all?" she says.

"You can't name everything."

She looks at me. I wait for her to smile, but she doesn't. She has decided that she doesn't even need to kill me. There are too many names, too many words, and they all have bits of silk attached to them like memories, like feelings, whatever. You name things, you feel things.

"There are too many names, too many words, too many passwords, too many bits of silk attached to things. Too many. You have to be . . . seductive. Selective."

Now she smiles. What's worse, she touches me. On the knee, though without any hammer. Softly. Almost gently. Bitch.

"Thank you," I tell her. "For the potted plants. If you will excuse me, I need to go now. Or I will be late for bingo."

Yet as soon as she is gone, I continue my experiment. What else am I going to do?

This time I sit in the window holding both my husbands in my lap. They have no names. You can't remember everything. Words are so, and names are too. All kinds of things are attached, like bits of silk. But bits of silk get mixed up, attached to the wrong door handles.

You can't remember every little thing. You can't feel every little thing.

"You must remember," they tell me, and, "Don't forget."

The nice boy in my diary wrote *forget*. Or *fuck it*, or something. No, I mean the nice boy wrote *forget*, or *fuck it*, or something, in my diary. The nice boy is not in the diary, obviously. The nice boy is nowhere, as far as I can tell. He has been stood down. Stood up, stood down. It's not as if he ever stood up, not really. Stood sideways, moved sideways, always moving away like his mop across the floor, his mop and his beautiful mop-like fringe. Standing, but not exactly up.

Why am I thinking about the nice boy, instead of the two husbands in my lap?

I need to what do you call it . . . *Ficus*. Focus.

I miss the nice boy. I miss our conversations. And my two husbands. Well, one of them I don't miss.

Forget-me-not. *Myosotis scorpioides*.

Should I remember? Or should I forget? Forget me, or forget me not?

The word in the diary was, if I remember, *forget*. But I don't remember to forget what, exactly. I don't exactly remember what to forget.

And there is a noise. A sound, at least, and a loud one at that. But I can't quite hear it. I can't quite make it here. If I can't hear it, is it a sound? If I have a password, and I don't know what it is, is it a password? If I had a husband, and I don't know his name, did I have a husband?

All this makes me very tired. I put both my husbands back on the whatsitsname. Perhaps I should just forget.

Let us forget.

Lettuce forget.

Forget lettuce. Forget *Lactuca sativa*. Forget *Myosotis scorpioides*. Forget *Corymbia maculata*. Forget *Rosa multiflora*. Forget Rose. Perhaps I should forget Rose, and Rose in the garden, and Rose in that garden with the older fellow and the lovely, rosy spots, and the sound, the sound I remember, the sound I can't quite hear. The sound that is not quite here.

Forget me, forget me not.

Perhaps I should just give up.

I do not give up. I continue. I sit in the wheelchair, at the window, and I continue my experiment. I hold the photo of the older fellow in my lap. I hold in my lap the photo of the older fellow. I look at the photo, then I look out the window.

Nothing but parking lot.

I persist.

Parking lot.

But there is a sound. I cannot quite hear it, but it is here. And something moves over the parking lot. A shape. A shadow. A bird.

I look more closely at the picture of the older fellow. I look, and I look.

I can hear the birds. What a noise they make.

And he is beside me in the garden, and he squeezes my hand.

There are forget-me-nots. *Myosotis scorpioides*.

There is lettuce. *Lactuca sativa*.

Gardenia magnifica.

Rosa arvensis. Rosa canina. Rosa multiflora.

There is laughter. There is birdsong. From songbirds. Perhaps there is birdlaughter. From laughterbirds.

Laughterbirds, wattlebirds, whipbirds, blackbirds, bellbirds, bowerbirds, butcher-birds, bristle-birds, grass-birds, dollar birds, catbirds, cicada birds, fig-birds, friarbirds, sunbirds, pilot birds, mistletoe birds, apostle birds.

Thornbills, spinebills, weebills, white-eyes, silvereyes, magpies.

Wagtails, fantails, firetails, needletails, bronzewings, lapwings, wheatears, whitefaces, frogmouths, scrubtits, nightjars.

Honeyeaters, flower-peckers, flycatchers, log runners, bee-eaters, tree creepers, kingfishers.

Whistlers, warblers, trillers, babblers.

Wrens, robins, wongas, wood swallows, finches, larks, thrushes, chats, choughs, drongos, koels, pardalotes, pittas, pipits.

Cuckoos, cuckoo shrikes, cuckoo doves, fruit doves, turtle-doves.

Currawongs, coucals, lorikeets, rosellas, king parrots, swift parrots, red-rumped parrots, cockatoos, cockatiels, corellas, gang-gangs, galahs.

What a noise there is.

There is birdsong.

There is laughter.

There is love.

I remember.

It's the laughter I remember. In love, in the garden, laughing.

He is beside me. On a garden bench, in sunshine. He holds my hand. He is older, but more recent, and on his neck he has lovely rosy spots, like roses. Rose and rows of roses. But he is not talking about roses, he is talking about lettuce.

"Lettuce," he says.

"Let us what?" I say.

He laughs.

"No," he says. "Lettuce. We should plant some."

"Cos?" I ask.

"Cos we both like eating it," he says, and I laugh, and he laughs, and the birds laugh too.

"Try to romaine calm," I tell him.

"Forget lettuce. I'm more of a rocket man."

"I don't carrot all."

"I suppose I'll just have to dill with it."

"Oh my Gourd."

"Speak now, or forever hold your peas."

"I love you. From my head tomatoes."

"And I love you. And time flies like an arrow, but fruit flies like a banana."

So, silliness. And love, laughter, birds, flowers. I remember it all. Despite the actual parking lot. And I remember those lovely rosy spots on his neck. Although I don't, actually, remember why I love them. Is it because they make it so clear, so maculately clear, that his neck is not that earlier neck, that previous neck, that neck of my first husband, that headless neck of the father of my children? That neck that rose up like a mountain, so high above Rose?

I feel the need to talk to the fellow who doesn't live here. It's about time. About time I let him know that he is not the only one: that I don't live here either, not really.

I find him in the dining room, looking at his meatballs.

I give him a number of opportunities, but he doesn't tell me that he doesn't live here.

"I think the meatballs are improving," he tells me.

It makes me feel like my heart might break.

"No, they're not," I tell him. "And they never will. And anyway, you don't live here. And I don't live here either. Not really."

You don't have to live here, I want to tell him. You don't have to do your living in this place. Even when they change your room, even when there is nothing but a parking lot in your window, even when they make changes to your account, even if you don't know your own password. Even here, even here in this place with the parking lot and the meatballs and the bingo, you don't have to be here, not really. You don't have to really live here. You can live, really, in your garden. You can have it, even if it isn't here. Or, in your case, if I remember, you can have your lovely white fence and your two-car garage.

"I quite like my room, really," he tells me, and he even talks about what floor his room is on, until I don't think I can take it anymore. On the wall above us, the smiling sharks grin at us with their nasty teeth and balance their awful beach balls on their horrible snouts.

"It's about time," he says, "for bingo." And he gets up from the table and walks away down the corridor, past the sign that says "Do Not Obstruct."

So I try to talk to my son and to my daughter. To reveal to them the results of my experiments.

To talk to them about love.

This does not go well.

I try to tell them about the wonderful garden and the laughter, the amazing noise of the birds, the incredible remembering of the names of things, the astounding beauty of those spots on the older fellow's neck.

Neither my daughter nor my son appears to feel that these things are wonderful, amazing, incredible, astounding. Neither. Nor.

But they do appear to feel something.

Not irritation, exactly, not annoyance. Not quite anger. Impatience, of course, and the usual degree of . . . incomprehension.

Something else.

Yet the more I try to share what I have discovered in my window, the more they both seem to feel this something and the less they seem able to hide this something they feel, and I have the feeling that hiding this something is something they have both managed to do until now, but now they can do it no more. Now that I try to talk to them about love, they can hide it no more.

So what is this feeling they feel?

Neither of them says it, neither of them will say its name, but in its way it is as loud as the noise of birds, or love.

Hurt. What do you call it. Resentment. Pain.

What they feel is pain.

I talk to them about love, and they feel pain.

Well, fuck them.

Ah, but I must be nice. And I must not forget the laughter. Even if it is that which annoys them most.

When I talk about the laughter, my son and my daughter both roll their eyeballs. Both of them. Just like Felicity and Charity. Only my son and my daughter do at least try to hide their eyeballs from me as they do it. My daughter by resting her forehead on the edge of the bathtub, my son by looking around the room the way he does.

Nevertheless, I don't stop talking about the laughter. Never the less. About how we made each other laugh, the older fellow and I. How we made the birds laugh. Finally, my son and my daughter can't take it any longer. Neither my son nor my daughter. Neither nor.

"His jokes," my daughter says softly, to herself or the bathtub or God.

"Laughing," says my son, to the ceiling, the walls, the furniture. "You and he were always laughing."

And I realize something. That my son and my daughter are never, neither my son nor my daughter are ever, present in that garden. That when I find my way through the window, past the parking lot, and into the garden, they are never there. When I find my way past the parking lot and into the past, my children are not present.

I should think about this.

I *must* think about this.

My children talk about the laughing, though what they really want to talk about is the forgetting. I don't want to talk about the forgetting. I do enough forgetting; I don't want to talk about it as well. What I want to talk about is the older fellow and the beautiful rosy spots on his neck.

But they go on and on about the forgetting.

"It's like you just forgot, Mom," one of them says.

Just forgot. Just. As though I haven't spent enough time and effort forgetting.

"Forgot what?" I say. "I don't remember any forgetting."

They roll their eyeballs again.

"As if you just forgot about our father," one of them says.

Which hardly seems fair, since I went to all the trouble of tearing off his head.

"As if you forgot about us," the other one says.

Or they don't say this, not exactly, but this is what they are saying when they say other things, about how the older fellow and I were always laughing, always in the garden laughing, just the two of us and the noisy birds and the flowers with all the names.

As if I could forget my own children. Their names, perhaps, but names come back, sometimes.

Rosa multiflora. Corymbia maculata. Eastern spinebill.

I must think about this.

I do not want to think about this.

What my children want, I think, is for me to name things.

But you name things, and then they are. They become. Sometimes, surely, it is best to leave things unnamed, so that they do not become. So that they are not. Or not so much, at least. And don't call me Shirley. Ha-ha, that's the medication.

You tie a piece of silk to something, and it becomes yours. But, also, you become it's. Its. Words are so. Names too.

My children. My son. My daughter. My husbands. One headless. One with laughter and beautiful spots.

It isn't only about remembering or forgetting.

There is forgetting, of course. And there is remembering, certainly. Nevertheless. Never the less.

There is the look in the eyes of my children as they look up at my headless husband as he tickles their little toes.

I know that look. I know what that look is.

It is love.

I must think about this.

I must think about this.

I love my children. Obviously I do. I never cut off their little toes, did I? Even when I removed their father's head.

But there was a time. A time when I turned away. Sometime after I turned away from their father, after I'd removed his head and after he'd been struck, stroked, stricken by his stroke.

Sometimes I wander, wonder about what time, exactly, this time was. Because it is time, I have even gone looking for it inside the big diary. But if it is there it must be hidden in one of the diary's secret places, the places that are not exactly there, perhaps written on one of those pages that have been removed by someone or something.

I do know that at the time my children were not children, exactly. Although, of course, children is exactly what they were.

And whatever that time was, it was at this time that I found myself in a garden, and with an entirely new husband.

And everything was different. The necks were different, I was different. I was in a garden. I was laughing. And there were no children.

I abandoned them. While they were grieving their lost father,

I abandoned them and spent my time with a new fellow, who surprisingly enough was an older fellow as well as more recent, and my children were left to tickle their own toes and to grieve over a headless photograph of their dead father.

So, nobody's perfect.

But what good abandoned children they are. For all their grievance about their grief and their abandonment, here they are every day, visiting their never entirely abandoned mother, and every day my son moves to the front the photograph of his mother's older and most recent fellow, and every day my daughter takes the potted plants and carries them into the bathroom for watering, or did until her mother threw them out the window into the parking lot.

What a son. What a daughter. What a mother.

So, like a mother, I think about my children.

They loved their father. Of course they did.

For all I know, he loved *them*. Of course he did.

For all I know, he loved *me*. Whatever.

How hurt they must have been. How bad I must have been, to hurt them so.

But. Nevertheless.

I did what I had to do.

And yet.

How good they are, these children. They do not turn away from me, as I turned away from them.

Every day, or most days, they come. They write in the big diary. They put potted plants in the bathtub. They take me somewhere nice for morning tea. They wash my revolting feet.

They also lie to me about money, true. They conspire with the Scare Manager and the Angry Nurse, true. When I'm not looking, they tie bits of silk to different door handles and they put parking lots in my window and they pretend that I know my password.

So, nobody's perfect.

My daughter, who doesn't know the name of a single plant and who has never heard a bird laugh and who could never be in a garden without it making her tired and who already has Felicity and Charity to keep her busy and make her suffer, my daughter nevertheless makes certain that my potted plants find their way into the bathtub. And even when I throw those potted plants out the window in a fit of age, rage, she still finds it in the depths of her tiredness to clean the bathtub, and even when I demand that she washes my rebellious toes she does it, and only sometimes sighs and only sometimes rests her head on the edge of the bathtub and prays to her God for her mother to die.

And my son with his thoroughly wiped bottom, my good son who comes every day or nearly every day depending on whether he has written it in the diary, and every time he comes he goes straight to the whatsitsname with all the pictures of the Dresser family on it and he pushes one photograph to the front. Not the one of his own father tickling the toes of he and his sister, of his sister and him, with both of them looking up with love and laughter at the mountainous neck of their father looking down lovingly and ticklingly and headlessly at them. No, the photo he moves to the front, for his mother's sake, is the one of the older fellow, the older yet more recent fellow with whom his own mother, who must have been a very bad mother indeed, went away to be in a garden and laugh and hold hands and to surround herself with flowers and bird noise instead of with her own children.

What good children they are. I must think about this. How much I have hurt them.

Nevertheless.

Never the less.

What I really want to think about is, are, the beautiful rosy spots on that older fellow's neck.

But first, there is that first husband.

About whom I wander. Wonder. My first, my headless husband. The father of my children. I wonder whether I killed him as well as cut off his head.

So I go looking in the big diary. I find a secret place where nothing is written, and I write down what I remember.

He always made me feel, to the extent that he made me feel, that I was a child, to a greater extent than our children. That I was, unlike our children, childish. Irresponsible. Inappropriate. And I was shellfish. Selfish. I was reckless. Without sufficient reck. Now, of course, although I may perhaps have no more reck than I had then, I am a wreck. I am filled with wreck. More wreckage than reckage, you might say.

"Rose," my dead husband would say to me, looking down at me from his mighty neck. Unless he called me something else. Perhaps it was darling or sweetheart, although that seems unlikely. Whichever word he used, in that one word were all the other words, the words for my many failings. My childishness, my irresponsibility, my selfishness, my recklessness. And his disappointment, his disapproval, his displeasure, his disgust, his dismay. And, in the end, his disappearance. Or not in the end, so much as in his head. In the end, the disappearance of his head.

Because if I didn't exactly kill him, I was certainly there when it happened. At the exact moment that he lost his head.

"Rose," he was saying, or whatever, from high above that neck of his, and I was ready to hear the list of my shortcomings. I didn't even need to look up all the way to his head, where it sat on top of his neck that rose like a mountain from its perfect collar and its tight-knotted tie. I knew what was to come.

And then it didn't come. Then there was nothing. As if he couldn't remember the words. Or as if he had run out of words to describe my failings, had exhausted his ability to express his disappointment in me.

I waited. The words would come, surely.

They didn't. He had stopped.

I looked up, all the way to the top of his neck, and there was nothing there. With one stroke it was all gone. The head of my husband had ceased, was silent. It was now just something that sat on top of his neck.

So I did the decent thing and removed it. No, that's just a euphorbia. Euphemism. What I did was tear it off, then at a later stage take a pair of scissors and trim along the ragged edge, removing his stricken head from that photograph of him looming lovingly over his two adoring children. Leaving the neck, of course, which was the main part of him anyway, even before the stroke. Or did I take off the top of that photograph beforehand? With my own hand? Had I struck before the stroke? Was that why he was stricken? Had I performed magic? Had I actually beheaded my children's father? Despite all my irresponsibility, was I, after all, responsible?

I forget.

What I remember is the older fellow. The older yet more recent fellow. It's about time.

Of course it's about those spots, but at first I don't even notice them, I don't even notice his neck. His neck doesn't matter. Imagine that.

What matters is the laughter. When I first enter the older fellow's garden, I am knocked over by the laughter. Laterally, literally, knocked over. The first time, or every time? Do I even remember the first time? I forget.

But I enter that garden of his, and I am knocked over. Head over heels. Head over, heals.

"Welcome to my garden," he says, and he invites me in through a great big, rusty, funny-looking gate. Invites me. Allows me. Encourages me.

I must tell the truth. I don't remember what that garden gate looks like. But there is a wall around that garden, I am sure, so there must be a gate. And everything outside that wall is just parking lot, I am certain of that.

Anyway, no sooner am I inside that gate, inside that garden, than I am knocked over. Everywhere there are leaves and flowers, most of which I do not know the names of and so have not yet forgotten. And there are birds, laughing. And one of them, a many-colored paraclete, parakeet, lorikeet, *Trichoglossus moluccanus*, flies straight at me, laughing. I try to avoid it. It keeps coming. I rear back, I duck, I duck back, like a backward duck, and on it comes, straight at my head as if I don't even have a head and all that lorikeet sees is empty space, open sky, and I am about to lose my head to a laughing bird and I rear back so far that I am on my back, on my rear, and that bird has flown straight through the space where my head was and continued on, laughing. And all the other birds in the garden are laughing, and the older fellow is laughing. And I too, toppling backward into the flowers, I am laughing, and the noise is everywhere, not just in my head. Head over heels. Head over, heals.

There are certain things that, at first, I don't notice. I do notice what a child he is, with his childish laughter and his silly jokes and his playfulness. How he plays with his spade and his garden fork and his whatsitsname, wheelbarrow, and his vegetables and all the trees and flowers he has so many silly names for, and how it all amazes me because I have always thought of gardening as dull housework, only dirtier. Yet this is such childish fun, and even when we rest in the sunshine of our garden bench we still play and hold each other's hands like children and make jokes about the names of things and even the birds laugh, and I give not one thought to my own fatherless children left at home with a headless photograph.

And then there is the first time that he squeezes my hand in the sunshine and there is the sound of him saying:

"I love you."

And the birds make such a noise, such a noise as I have never heard before, and then I realize that the noise is me, and I am saying:

"And I love you."

But then, this is the thing. I begin to worry about him. What I worry about is his neck.

It's about time. For some time, I barely notice his neck. Imagine that. What I notice is how much younger the older fellow is. Or more childlike, anyway. He likes to be naughty and silly, like a child. Not like *my* children, obviously.

"Listen," he says. "Look. Can you see it? It's a gang-gang!"

"What's a gang-gang?" I ask, expecting one of his jokes.

"It's a cockatoo. Have you ever seen one?"

"I've seen a cockatoo," I say.

"I bet you have," he says, and he's laughing so hard that I understand.

"You terrible man. What I mean is I have only ever seen an ordinary cockatoo."

"There's no such thing as an ordinary cockatoo," he says, suddenly almost serious.

Together we look at the beautiful bird, laughing the whole time.

"It's very beautiful," I say. "And rare, surely?"

"Rare, and well-done. So much is at steak. And don't call me Shirley."

That laughter. Those jokes.

It's not as if he laughs out loud all the time or tells knock-knock jokes while he's working in the garden, making silly puns while he turns the compote, compost, with his long-handled bitchfork, bitchfuck, pitchfork.

It's not as if he laughs all the time like a lunatic, or a lorikeet.

It's not as if he thinks everything is funny, exactly. But he sees that things are not serious, not in the way that other people think everything is serious. Or he sees that everything is serious in a whole nother way. Nother. Another, whole way. A hole way, when he's digging holes. When he's spreading mulch. Thank you very mulch, he'll say. *Corymbia maculata*. Our Lady of the Maculate Conception. *Myosotis scorpioides*. Forget-me-not. Fuck it, why not?

He is different because he sees how everything is the same. Or not the same, but connected. Like the bright sound of the sunshine and the multicolored laughter flying straight at your head like a lunatic lorikeet.

He likes things to be silly. Even planting lettuces, even pruning roses. And he wonders. He doesn't only wonder at the rose, he wonders at the prune.

"Prune," he says, with the sex tours in his hand. Secateurs. "I wonder why it's *prune*? Why not *plum*? Plumbing the depths of *Rosa multiflora*? I wonder how *prune* arose? I'm just raisin the question. I don't have an answer, currantly."

Or we'll be admiring the Cootamundra wattle and its impossibly beautiful golden flowers. *Acacia baileyana*.

"Wattle one say about such a beautiful thing? Wattle one compare it to? That's what I ask myself, acacianally."

Ha-ha. All without medication. His jokes are so bad, and I love them so much.

It's as if he has the ability to tickle his own toes.

And then I begin to worry about his neck. As if I am responsible. As if I am the responsible one. I worry, responsibly, about all the time he spends in the sun. I tell him to wear a hat, remind him about skin cancer, just like I must have done with my children, although I don't remember it. I notice his neck, and how there are spots on it. Small red spots. Are they getting bigger? Shouldn't he have them checked? But he only laughs and says he prefers spots to checks, *maculata* to harlequin, motley to plaid.

"Glory be to God for dappled things," he says, "for skies of couple-color as a brinded cow, for rose-moles all in stipple upon trout that swim."

Gerard Manley Hopscotch, he tells me.

He laughs at the words even as he throws them about like bright spots of confetti in the sunshine. He laughs at the most serious things, as he does at the most beautiful things. He takes to calling those rosy spots on his neck his rose-moles, and as they grow he laughs about his rows and rows of rosy rose-moles competing with his roses, his multiplying neck-roses, his very own *Rosa multiflora*.

At last I am able to persuade him to have his spots checked, to submit to a spot check.

And it turns out that they are nothing. According to the doctors, there is nothing on his neck. Nothing to fear, nothing of importance.

"Thank God," I say.

"For dappled nothings," he says.

"For things of no importance," I say.

And I have never seen anything so beautiful as those spots. It makes me laugh like a lorikeet, a great noise of lunatic laughter. That something can be so beautiful because it is not something else.

It is only later that I learn what else the doctors told him.

The Peloponnesian girl gives me a cup of tea with my medication, calls me dear, and hits my knee with a tiny hammer.

The Angry Nurse is everywhere, smiling and threatening everyone with her clipboard.

The Scare Manager has a bright, shiny new motorcycle, which he rides into the parking lot wearing a bright, shiny helmet like a bank robber, or a gang-gang cockatoo, only it's the wrong color. It appears to be made of gold. He leaves it on the desk in his office. The helmet, not the motorcycle. It sits beside the paperwork on his desk like a big round golden idiot. Ingrate. Ingot. He also has a new gold earring. He keeps this in his ear, not in his eyebrow or his nose or his mouth, like the nice boy who once mopped the floors.

My son has meetings with the Scare Manager in his office, with the door closed. I don't exactly spy on them, but I notice that some days when I happen to be outside the Scare Manager's office with my ear against the door there is nothing written in the big diary about my son coming to visit. So I write it in the diary myself, and the next time my son does come to visit me he seems surprised when he reads that he has been in the Scare Manager's office having a secret meeting about my account. I tell him that perhaps there is something wrong with his memory, so just as well we have the big diary, and my son looks around the room the way he does and tells me I trust him, don't I, and I say of course I do, and he seems to become more relaxed and lies to me some more about money. Then I tell him I like the Scare Manager's new leather jacket and how well it goes with his golden turtle and my son looks nervous again, and everything is normal, or at least usual.

My daughter is very, very tired. She has brought me a new potted plant. She is so good that I haven't the heart to tell her I don't need potted plants anymore, because of the garden. She takes the new potted plant into the bathroom, where she kneels beside the bathtub and sighs. It is not really the potted plant, or God, that makes her so tired. It is Felicity and Chastity, who, now that they have had their Graduation Ball, are about to have their final exams. Felicity, or Chastity, is still having problems with biology. Both of them are busy studying on their smart phones. Judging by the speed of their thumbs, they will do very well. Final exams now have a new name, like so many other things. They are now called Schoolies, and require much research. They are held in a penthouse instead of a schoolhouse, and are very expensive. The subject makes my daughter rest her forehead on the edge of the bathtub.

Felicity and Chastity are such good girls that, even though they have been so busy, they have nevertheless kept their promise to their Granma to find out news about the nice boy who mops the floors. He won't be at Schoolies, they tell me. He didn't go to the Grad Ball, they tell me. Some problem about a lack of trans-friendly toilet facilities, they tell me. I don't know if this is to do with his mop or not. Then they tell me that they have heard he was attacked, beaten up by transphobes.

"Attacked?" I say. "Beaten? Up? Train probes?"

They ignore me. I don't blame them. The thought of the nice boy being hurt is so . . .

"It's so wrong," says Felicity.

"Everybody can be whatever they want to be," says Chastity.

That can't be right, I think, but don't say anything. I want to hold the nice boy. To hold him close and to tell him . . . what? To forget?

Then they tell me it's okay, he's been getting support, and they have encouraged all their friends to like him on the face tube. They are such good girls.

"Word is," says Felicity, "he's doing a community college course in something or other."

"IT," says Chastity.

"Eye tea?" I say. "With real eyeballs? That can't be very nice, surely?"

They make it clear that they don't have time for my silly games.

"Tech, Granma," they say, and roll their own eyeballs and waggle their smart phones to illustrate the whole range of widely understood things that are beyond my what do you call it.

"Information technology," they say. "Data processing."

"And he'll be back here working," says Felicity.

"One day a week," says Chastity.

"On probation," says Felicity. "Strictly limited interaction with residents."

They know so much. So, he has not forgotten me. Bless him. Even though he wrote *forget* in my diary, he has not forgotten me.

"Why are you so interested, Mom?" my daughter asks from the bathtub, making it clear that my interest is yet another thing she has to deal with.

"I think he knows," I say, somewhat to my surprise.

"Knows? Knows what? What does he know?"

"I forget."

This appears to satisfy her.

And then, when I am wondering on the ground floor with my walker, I see the nice boy, with his mop. I almost laugh out loud like some kind of lorikeet. The floor he mops is near the doorway to the IT lounge. Perhaps he is doing computers as well as mopping floors. Perhaps that is why they have allowed the nice boy back. Perhaps he mops the computers as well as the floors. I hope the computers are friendlier than the toilets.

I move my walker toward him, I smile, but he shrinks away sideways toward the nearest "Do Not Obstruct" sign. I don't blame him. He has bruises on his face, and it appears that someone has torn the earrings from his nose and eyebrows. And his breasts seem smaller, somehow. As if they are not getting support, or are not being liked. I like them, of course, but I don't have a face tube.

The nice boy's face is darker than I remember. Or is it his eyes that are darker? Or is it that they are more made up? With makeup, I mean, not made up like the things my son says about my account. Made up to hide the bruises he received in those unfriendly toilets.

I move closer, but he moves farther away, retreating. Or retweeting, as Felicity and Charity would say. Then I think he is perhaps not retweeting at all so much as inviting me to follow. So I do. Until there we are, up against the big doors together, under the "Do Not Obstruct" sign, obstructing.

"I've missed you," I tell him.

He almost looks at me.

"Careful," he says, I think.

"Shit," I say, then, "Fuck," just to let him know I understand. Then I ask, "Did they hurt you very much?"

"Fuck it," he says, or, "Forget it."

And I see that he has tried to flatten those breasts of his, has bound them tight with something. Wrapped them with bandages, like a mummy or the old Invisible Man from TV. It makes me feel so sad.

"You can be whatever you want to be," I say.

This time he does look at me.

"Fuck," he says.

I take his point.

And then I take his hand. I put my hand on his hand, both our hands on the mop handle, and I look at his dark, bruised eyes, and I see there is something in them. Something that is not exactly light, not exactly bright, but is somehow connected to light, as flowers are connected to sunshine, as birds are connected to laughter. Something growing. Put him in a garden, I think, that's what he needs. More than even the friendliest of toilets.

I hold his hand. He holds the mop handle. He doesn't try to move away, not exactly. He mumbles something.

"Urine," it might be.

I look down to check, but my pantsuit seems fine.

"You're in," he says. "Danger."

And then I see the Angry Nurse coming toward us. I see her see our hands joined on the mop handle. She smiles. I take my hand away. The nice boy makes a sort of sound, like a cry half-swallowed.

"Is there something I can do for you, dear?" the Angry Nurse says.

Then she turns to the nice boy.

"Shouldn't you be somewhere?" she says.

"I was just asking him what day the next quiz night is on," I say.

But the nice boy has already shrunk away, slid away sideways with his mop, shriveled away like that something in his eyes.

The Angry Nurse smiles.

The fellow who doesn't live here is afraid. I find him sitting in a wheelchair against the wall, beneath the smiling sharks, doing his best to look inconsiderate, inconspicuous. The Hittite girl has just put a nice cup of tea in his lap, which he spills all over himself when I say hello.

As always, the fellow who doesn't live here knows what's going on.

"I know what's going on," he tells me.

"What's going on?" I ask him.

"Don't you see what's happening?" he asks me.

"Happening?"

"There's a shake-up," he says.

"A shake?" I say, just to clarify. "Up?"

I just want him to tell me he doesn't live here.

"There's more," he says. "There's always more."

I wonder if he's talking about the meatballs.

"It's all about the numbers," he says, so perhaps it's bingo.

He's becoming more and more what do you call it. He spills more tea in his lap. He signals to me that we might be overheard, that someone might be listening.

Trust me, I want to tell him, no one is listening.

"Things are changing," he says. So, it's not about the meatballs.

"I am being transitioned," he tells me.

I tell him I know exactly how he feels, which doesn't seem to help.

"You have to keep paying," he says. "More and more and more."

I want to ask him what this has to do with sitting against the wall in a wheelchair under a bunch of stupid sharks bouncing beach balls on their nasty snouts, but of course I know the answer: that if you don't keep paying more and more you'll get transitioned, Holistically, and before you know it you'll find yourself in a strange room with the same piece of silk on the wrong door handle, or sitting in a wheelchair against the wall with a puddle of tea in your lap, or falling out your window and ending up on your back in the parking lot, staring at the sky.

"Because there's always someone who can pay more," he says.

"It's all okay," I tell him. "It's Best Practice. It's Person-Centered. I have an account. And a password. And a good son who looks after everything."

I hate to lie to the fellow who doesn't live here, but what
can I do?

I must think about this. I must think about what I can do.
There must be something.

Then something happens in my room. Something happens in my
bed. Not my actual room, obviously, not my actual bed, but the
room where the fellow with the nasty lines on his neck lies in my
old bed with his mouth and his pajamas open and doesn't look at
my window with the leaves and trees in it but at the TV high on the
wall. The room that I know is my room because it doesn't have a
piece of silk tied to the door handle or a parking lot in the window.

I sit beside him, suggest Scrabble, but he just stares at the TV.

"I don't like you," I remind the nasty fellow, just to be clear.

But he only stares at the TV, where important-looking fellows
are leaving an important-looking building, and less important
persons are pointing microscopes, microphones at them. The important ones appear to be politicians or criminals, child molesters
or archbishops. I don't care about any of it. I watch a fly crawl
along one of those nasty lines on his neck. Another fly peers into
the nasty hole in his pajamas, as if it's looking for a password.

"Things are changing," I tell him. I want something to happen. I am reminded of my headless husband, with his mighty
neck. I had wanted something to happen, and then it happened.

"Change is good," I say.

I think of the older fellow and how much I love those beautiful spots of his, which are not skin cancer.

"Or not," I add.

And I think of the fellow who doesn't live here, sitting
against the wall beneath the sharks, being transitioned.

"I know what's going on," I say, because what the fuck, he's
not listening anyway. "I know you can afford to pay. I've seen the
pile of gold on the Scare Manager's desk."

The TV shows policemen who don't look like policemen, holding an important fellow by the arms, leading him toward a police car that doesn't look like a police car. Then they help the important fellow into the back seat, being very careful that he doesn't bump his head, so you know they are policemen and that it is a police car.

"But there's always more," I say.

That fellow on the TV reminds me of someone.

"You always have to pay more," I say.

There are drops of sweat on his face. They run along his chin. They slide into the nasty lines on his neck. A fly takes a little drink.

The TV changes to a fellow who looks like the fellow with the policemen but some time before. He is laughing and waving a bottle of . . . champagne, then he is cutting a big ribbon with a pair of golden scissors, then he has his arm around some other famous fellow, then there is more champagne, there are beautiful young women, more important-looking buildings. He seems to be a very successful gangster, or a politician. Then the TV returns to the police car and there he is, in the back seat, as it drives slowly away. He doesn't look out the window, just bows his head toward his knees. The feeling that comes from the TV is shame, defeat, downfall.

And I see now it isn't sweat on the fellow who lies there in my bed. Not drops of sweat that slide along his cheek and fall down from his chin to run like nasty little rivers in the furrows of his neck. They are tears.

The fly drinks them anyway.

He is crying. He is weeping. He is sobbing.

I know who the fellow on the TV reminds me of.

Then his mouth, still open and focused on the TV, changes shape enough to make a sound.

"Sun," he says.

And, of all things, I want to tell him that it's all right. That it's okay. That the sun is good, that sunshine in a garden is beautiful.

But no. Not sun.

"Son. My son."

Now, if there is one thing I don't care about, it's other people's sons.

But.

Except.

Nevertheless.

The tears are streaming out of him now, running in rivers down his neck, and of all the strange things which seem to be happening, the strangest is that I am holding his hand.

"I'm so sorry," I tell him.

He is silent again. Silent, and sobbing. And on the silent TV, the car drives silently away with his son in the back seat, head bowed, between two silent policemen.

I hold his hand. There are just the two of us. And the flies.

"I have a son too," I tell him, in case it helps. "That's what you need in this place. A good son, with a thoroughly wiped bottom. Who knows your password, who looks after your account."

It doesn't help. Of course it doesn't. His son won't be looking after any accounts for a while. Perhaps that's why the police have taken him away. They have discovered something unpleasant about his bottom. They know his password. They know everything. That's why they are so crapulous in their duty of care. Scrofulous. Scrupulous. The way they fold him into that police car, the way they put their hands so carefully on his head to help him through the police car door, the way they drive him slowly away with his password and his shame. It is Best Practice. It meets Performance Benchmarks, going forward.

There's always more. You always have to pay more. There's always someone.

He is still crying.

I try a different approach.

"It's Holistic," I say. "It's Person-Centered."

It doesn't help.

I hold his hand.

The fly looks into his pajamas.

And I try again to tell him about the sunshine in the garden, about the noise of the birds and about the older fellow and his silly jokes and about being knocked over by a lorikeet and about saying "*I love you.*"

This doesn't help either. I sit there, and I hold his hand. It is enough.

He knows. I know. We both know. It is something we both know, like a password.

Finally, long after the police have driven away his son in the police car with all his passwords and accounts and all his ability to keep on paying more, the Angry Nurse arrives, as I knew she would.

What do I care? What do I care about this nasty fellow with flies all over his neck and inside his pajamas? What do I care about his gang-gang, gangster son, his sunny boy, his very own sonny Jim, being driven away along with his ability to keep on paying more? What do I care about this nasty old fellow not being able to pay more anymore? What do I care if that means he'll be transitioned, like the rest of us?

The Angry Nurse looks at the two of us. Him with his mouth open, with the fly drinking the tears from his neck, and another fly looking into the open fly of his pajamas. And me, holding his hand.

The Angry Nurse smiles.

The next day, when I'm wondering in the corridor, I see the Scare Manager go into that room, the same room with no silk on the door handle. Very quietly I follow, close enough to see him turn off the TV and do something with the fellow's pillows while he talks to him, low and close like a fly crawling over his neck. When the Scare Manager looks back toward the doorway I see a flash of gold from his turtle, like a warning, and I shuffle away fast with my walker. Not long after he leaves, I see the Angry

Nurse go into the room. When she comes out, she is carrying a pillow.

I know what that pillow is. I've watched enough TV. It's evidence.

I go into the room after her. His mouth is open. His eyes are open. His pajamas are open.

He is as dead as the TV.

I need to tell my son about my discoveries. I need to tell my daughter. I must talk to my children, tell them what I have learned.

What is it I have learned?

The learning. The understanding. The danger.

I need my children to understand. To understand, I need my children.

My friend on her back in the parking lot. The fellow with the lines on his neck, which were really not so nasty, with his open mouth and pajamas, who cried for his son and whose hand I held. The Angry Nurse and the pillow.

So now there must be someone else. Someone who can pay more. Someone whose account may be accessed, to add to the pile of gold on the Scare Manager's desk.

Always more. Never the less.

None of which is important. What is important is the loss. The losing.

I am making no sense, obviously.

My daughter rests her head on the edge of the bathtub and sighs.

My son looks around the room the way he does.

I keep trying. I tell them that I need to tell them about my discoveries.

"What have you discovered, Mom?" my daughter asks, making it clear that she is too busy and too tired for the answer. She scrubs away at the bathtub. If she could find another potted plant, she would water it. She may well wash my feet before she's finished. Felicity and Charity aren't with her today, only God. Felicity and Charity are partying, now that their exams are over.

"Partying," my daughter says, as if the word suggests everything that is the opposite of my bathtub, and of God.

"I think Chastity has a boyfriend," she says, as though it is the final whatsitsname. Straw.

"So, she's no longer having problems with biology?"

My daughter sighs.

"Mom, there is nothing to discover," my son tells me when he sees what I have written in the big diary.

"That doesn't sound right," I tell him, and I try as cutely, acutely, accurately as I can to describe how the fellow in my bed died after I held his hand, after his important gangster son was driven away by the police so that he wouldn't hurt his head and the Scare Manager came to talk to him unguently, urgently, about the piles of gold and the placement of his pillows, after which the Angry Nurse arrived and then left carrying a pillow, after which the TV and the fellow in my bed were both dead.

My son looks around the room as if he hasn't understood a single word I've said. Then he says, "You trust me, Mom, don't you?"

So I know he does understand, except in all the ways he doesn't. He is such a good son. Just as good as any important gang-gang son. I wonder if they know each other? My son with his thoroughly wiped bottom and the dead fellow's son with his thoroughly protected head? Both of them helping the Scare Manager to reach his Best Practice Benchmarks, going forward.

But different too, these good sons. One of them an important gangster on the TV, one of them with cash flow hiccups. One of them passing gangster money to the Scare Manager so that his father has the best room and the best window, one of them lying to his mother about her account so that the Scare Manager gets to launder his golden turtles and the son gets his cash flowing and his mother gets her piece of silk tied to a different door handle and a parking lot in her window. One of them driven away by the police so that his father suddenly has a pillow problem, one of them pretending that his mother doesn't have a password problem so that he can solve his hiccup problem and make certain that the Scare Manager has no golden turtle problem, going forward.

But none of this is important. What is important is the loss. What is important is the losing.

And, somehow, the being careful with heads. How the police are so careful with the head of the gangster son as they drive him away. How my good son so carefully tucks his mother and her walker into his little car when he takes her somewhere nice for morning tea. Perhaps this also is what the police are doing when they drive away the dead fellow's son? Taking him somewhere nice for morning tea? That seems unlikely. But people are certainly careful with other people's heads.

My son is careful, certainly, with his mother's head. Or of what's inside it. And what is it that's inside it? Is it her password? I should protect my password, my son tells me. My son is so careful to protect my password that he won't even let me know what it is.

I am so proud of him. He may not be a famous gangster, but he does his best. He visits me almost every day, writes in the big diary so I don't forget, sometimes takes me somewhere nice for morning tea even though he hates doing it, and goes to all the trouble of lying to me about my account.

And as if that isn't enough, every day when he comes to visit he pushes the photo of the older fellow right to the front, in front of all the other Dresser family photos. Even though the older fellow is not his father. Even though his father is the headless fellow whose head was torn off while he played with his children's toes.

Of course, I am proud too of my daughter and all her work with bathtubs and with Felicity and Charity. But she has her God, as well as Felicity and Charity. My son only has his cash flow and his thoroughly wiped bottom. And my account.

But it is the loss. The losing. Something about the older fellow with the lovely spots on his neck, those lovely spots on his neck that are not cancer, in the garden with the laughter and the noise and the holding of hands.

And how I held the hand of the dead man who lay in my bed, in my room, as he watched his son being driven carefully away, while flies crawled in the lines on his neck, which in the end were not so nasty. I held his hand and he died. I held his hand, and there was love, and then he died. Not love between me and the dead man, of course. Between the dead man and his son. And the loss. The losing. The transitioning.

So, necks. Holding hands. Loss.

And my son and my daughter.

The older fellow in the garden never played with the toes of my children.

The older fellow had nothing to do with my children. And my children had nothing to do with him or his garden.

It is the loss, the losing.

My first husband lost his head.

My children lost their headless father.

I found the older fellow, and the garden, and the love.

My children did not.

For me, the love.

For them, the loss.

I am not, obviously, a good mother.

And yet they come to visit me and they write in the big diary and they kneel beside the bathtub and they look after my account and they wash my toes and water my potted plants and take me somewhere nice for morning tea and move the photo of the older fellow, who did not love them, to the front of all the other Dresser family photos, and they leave at the back the photo of their headless father, who did.

What good children they are.

It's as if they are being careful with my head. With their bad old mother's head.

And yet.

Nevertheless.

And yet, nevertheless, I am in danger.

"I love those lovely spots on your neck," I say to the older fellow in the garden.

He holds my hand, laughing.

"Of course you do," he says. "They are my most lovable feature."

"They are not skin cancer," I say.

"Yes," he says. "They are not skin cancer. That is exactly what they are not."

There is laughter, sunshine, the noise of birds.

Something is wrong.

"Tell me one of your terrible jokes."

He only laughs.

I do not remember him ever not laughing. I do not ever remember him not laughing. I do not remember him not laughing, ever.

Also I do not remember him, ever, speaking of my children.

Also I do remember me never speaking of my children. Never.

It is something I remember us not doing together.

Because there is only us. Only the two of us and the sunshine and the laughter.

Another thing I do not remember, apart from my children, is the older fellow's children. Or his wife. His earlier wife, obviously. I know that he has an earlier wife, as well as children, because he never mentions them. This is not unlike a piece of silk on a door handle.

We forget together. It is just us. Only us, ever.

Perhaps it is this that is wrong.

Or perhaps it is that, although he laughs, he no longer makes his jokes. His silly, lovable jokes.

"Tell me a joke," I say.

He laughs.

"Look at that beautiful acacia," I say. "I wonder, wattle they think of next?"

He laughs.

"I saw a beautiful gang-gang, flying over the herb garden," I say. "But of course, you and I have both seen a cockatoo, in our thyme."

"Ha-ha," he says. "Ha."

Nevertheless, he no longer makes his own terrible jokes about the names of things. He no longer names things. Never. The less. Not only children. Cockatoos too. No more *Callocephalon fimbriatum*. No more golden wattle, *Acacia pycnantha*. Perhaps what he needs is a piece of silk attached to everything. Even things that don't quite seem to exist, like other people, or children.

It is here that I remember.

"What else did those doctors tell you, after they told you those beautiful spots weren't cancer?"

He doesn't laugh, he only squeezes my hand.

"I forget," he says.

"Try," I tell him.

"No," he says. "That is what the doctors told me. That I forget. That I am forgetting. And that I will forget. Everything. Now it is the names of things. Soon it will be the things. Every thing. Everything."

I look at his neck and the beautiful spots, which are not cancer. And I look above his neck at what else those doctors saw, which was worse. When they saw the forgetting. And now I see it too. And even though this is before the time of pieces of silk on my own door handles, I want to tie a piece of silk to the older fellow. But even though this is earlier, nevertheless I know that it is already too late for pieces of silk. It is too late for everything. Never. The less.

So we sit, holding hands in the garden, and there is only the noise of birds.

I am afraid," I tell my son.

"I am in danger," I tell my daughter.

I know what will happen to me.

The Angry Nurse has been here with her clipboard and has smiled at me and hit my knee with a tiny hammer and the Taliban girl has given me a nice cup of tea with my new medication and suggested that it might be even nicer for me to sit closer to the window, out of which is the parking lot.

The Angry Nurse has been paying close attention to my pillows.

"Let me rearrange your pillows, dear," she says, and she smiles.

"You don't frighten me," I tell her, but we both know it isn't true.

We understand each other.

She is choosing the pillow, since I refuse to sit close enough to the window for their purposes. And soon the Scare Manager will be here, and there will be the whatsitsname. The transitioning.

After which the Angry Nurse will return to remove the evidence. Perhaps, beside the pile of gold in the Scare Manager's office, there is also a growing pile of pillows.

But none of this is important, not really. What I am really afraid of is the forgetting. There is always more.

"I forgot you," I tell my children.

At least I try to. But they appear not to hear me.

I try nevertheless.

"I am sorry," I want to say. "I have not been a good mother. And you have been such good children. You have been good to your bad mother. You have never abandoned me. Nevertheless, I abandoned you, after cutting off the head of your father, who loved you. Your mother cut off your father's head while he was playing with your toes, and then forgot you with an older fellow in a garden who loved her, until he forgot too. Until he, too, forgot. And I am sorry, but I had love, and it was not just goodness. It was laughter and sunshine and the noise of birds."

I am getting nowhere.

"You are both so good to me. I do not forget that. Although I did forget you once. And I will again."

They don't hear me. As if I'm not here.

My daughter sighs. My son looks around the room. In their own way they have forgotten me. Abandoned me to their goodness, to their duty, to their care. It is, I suppose, a loving sort of revenge.

I would like them to know that I do not blame them for this. For being such good children that they make me invisible with their dutiful, vengeful love.

I would like to let my son know that I do not mind that he lies to me and steals from me. And reassure my daughter that she need not feel guilty about hating me while she cleans my bathtub and washes my feet.

I would like to tell them that there is always more. That my son might regain his cash flow and overcome his hiccups, but he will never be free of the Scare Manager. That the Scare Manager will never have enough gold, that there will always be someone who can pay more. That my son's bottom will never be entirely clean.

That my daughter can never water every potted plant, scrub every bathtub, that she and her God can wash all the feet in the world but there will always be more, and nothing can stop her own children, her very own Charity and Felicity, from one day scrubbing *her* bathtub and washing *her* toes and abandoning their mother to their own good, dutiful love.

Because, my children, there is always more. You both look after me so well, for all your lies and resentments. Even though I was your mother and I forgot you. But you are not all she forgot. There is always more. There is always someone. There is always something.

There is always more.

The fear and the danger do not stop me wondering the corridors with my walker. But I am stopped, and surprised, when I come across the nice boy who mops the floors embracing the fellow who doesn't live here. The nice boy's mop leans nearby, against the "Do Not Obstruct" sign.

The fellow who doesn't live here is writhing, whinnying, whimpering in his wheelchair, looking incontrovertible. Inconsolable. The nice boy is bending over him, consoling him. Or at least holding him. I am not sure that I have ever seen such tenderness.

"I am lost," says the fellow who doesn't live here.

"Fuck, shit, arsehole," says the nice boy, possibly.

"I don't know where I am," says the fellow who doesn't live here.

Actually, we are very close to the IT lounge.

"You don't live here," I tell him, only trying to help. It doesn't help, so I continue. "You have a nice white fence, a two-car garage, a lawn mower, a what do you call it . . . shape-shifter, shirt-lifter. Leaf blower."

But he remains inconceivable.

"Everything is changing," he says.

Well, obviously. What is most amazing to me is the way the nice boy holds him. Not sliding away sideways the way he usually does, but leaning in and wrapping the fellow who doesn't live here in his arms, enclosing him, or at least the top of him above the wheelchair, draped over the fellow's inconceivable head with his skinny arms wrapped around his whimpering shoulders, consoling him, conceiving of him.

The nice boy's bruises seem to have faded, but I see as he bends down to the fellow who doesn't live here that his bosom is bound tight to his chest. And I see that even though he is trans and doesn't have a single toilet that is friendly to him, and even though, according to Felicity and Charity, he is somewhere on that colored thing, the spectrum, although of course it is wrong to say *colored*, he holds the fellow who doesn't live here with such tender understanding, holding him close to his hidden bosom, being careful with his poor old head and whispering gently into his ear:

"Fuck, fuck, fuck."

Forget, forget, forget.

The nice boy reminds me of a long, soft piece of silk draped over the fellow who doesn't live here, helping him to see where he belongs and where he doesn't.

It is a beautiful thing to see. Not that it stops the fellow who doesn't live here from complaining about living here.

"Everything is changing," he says.

"Fuck it," the nice boy whispers into his ear.

"I need to check my account," says the fellow who doesn't live here, and I wonder whether the wonderful tenderness of the nice boy is really of any help to him at all. Perhaps the nice boy should be embracing me instead, draping himself over me like a beautiful piece of silk. I'm sure it would do me good. It would certainly do me no harm.

"I must know the truth," says the fellow who doesn't live here, and he looks at me as if he believes, even with the nice boy holding him so amazingly, that it is me, I, who can help him.

"You should not obstruct," I tell him, because right now I'm afraid as well as amazed.

"Fuck it," says the nice boy. So tenderly, gently, truthfully.

"The truth," the fellow who doesn't live here says. "The truth will save me."

I almost laugh.

"Oh, I don't think so," I say. He certainly has some strange ideas.

The nice boy seems to agree with me.

"Fuck it," he says. "Motherfucker."

Yet the fellow who doesn't live here is determined, as well as whimpering.

"All you need is the password," he says.

Well, yes. I think I liked him more when he didn't live here.

We can't stay out here in the open, obstructing. So we move along the corridor toward the IT lounge. What a sight we must be. The fellow who doesn't live here, in his wheelchair, whimpering about the truth, looking like some lost soul. The nice boy with his mop and his secret breasts, looking like no toilet would ever have him. And me, looking.

One of the computers has a sign on it that says "Out of Order." The other one has its usual picture of a mountain with snow, until the nice boy touches the piano, Scrabble board, keyboard, and it changes to a brightly lit slot that winks at us, waiting for its password. Gently the nice boy pushes the fellow and his wheelchair right up close, being careful with his head, encouraging him.

"Get fucked," he says. "Arsehole."

The fellow who doesn't live here hardly needs such encouragement. He whinnies lovingly at that little winking slot, as though he would climb in there and disappear if he could.

I can hardly stand to watch. I open one of the old . . . encyclopedias dumped against the wall in the corner. I look at Masada, Massachusetts, Mastodon, Mustard. Then Xanthorrhoea, Xerxes, Xylophone.

And I keep an eye on the corridor. The fellow who doesn't live here is still whimpering over his precious password, looking for his life or the truth or something, when I see the Angry Nurse and the Manichean girl hurry past. The Angry Nurse carries a pillow. Someone else has been murdered, I suppose, or is about to be.

I am afraid. Of course I am.

The older fellow in the garden looks at me, and squeezes my hand. Or, no, not really. I squeeze his hand. He just sits there.

"The doctors, or whatever they are. What is it that they told you?"

But I know, of course. Of course, I know.

"I forget," says the older fellow.

"Of course you do," I tell him, and I squeeze his hand. "I forget too."

"Forget to what?" he says. I laugh.

"No," I say. "I too forget. I forget, also."

"No," he says.

"We will forget together," I say, and squeeze his hand.

"No," he says.

There is only the sunshine, and the birds.

"Your name," he says.

"What about it?" I say, hoping for a joke.

"I forget," he says.

It's not much of a joke.

"I forget your name," he says.

There is just the sunshine, just the noise of the birds. I squeeze his hand.

"What is your name?" he says. He doesn't laugh, he doesn't even cry.

And there are roses. All around us are roses. *Rosa arvensis. Rosa canina. Rosa multiflora.*

"Rose," I say. It is as good a name as any.

"My name is Rose," I tell him.

I think he believes me.

Sunshine. Birds. Roses.

So, it seems, we will forget together.

And we will sit here together, in the time that is left, holding hands.

We will understand each other.

He has shown me many things, but it is this I must remember. He has made me understand about understanding. Perhaps he was a teacher too. I don't know what he was.

Yet for a time he was everything.

The fellow who doesn't live here is beside himself. Not really, of course. It is the nice boy who is beside him, helping him look into that computer, being careful with his head. While here I am in the corner with my pile of tattered old encyclopedias. Empiricism. Entrainment. Enchilada. Entrepreneur.

They are so close, those two, as if they are inside that computer together, getting closer and closer to the truth. Or something.

Perhaps I am jealous. The nice boy should be close to me instead, being careful with my head, calling me motherfucker and telling me to fuck off in that sweet, tender way of his.

Nevertheless. It doesn't help the fellow who doesn't live here. They get close, but not close enough. The fellow who doesn't live here, for all his efforts, stays lost. He can't find his life or the truth or whatever.

He slumps, defeated. The computer turns into a mountain again.

The nice boy holds him close. Consolidates him, consoles him, telling him gently, tenderly, to fuck off, fuck it, forget.

Outside in the corridor the Angry Nurse roams, looking for pillows.

Even worse, here comes the Scare Manager. He is Holistic.

"Repeated warnings," he says. "Fragrant disregard of."

Behind him, the Angry Nurse smiles. She has a clipboard, and a pillow.

"Care," he says. "Duty of. Staff–Client Interaction Protocols, contravention of. Probationary Employment Pathway, immediate termination of. Person-Centered Scare Plan, reassessment of. Meatballs, consumption of. Turtles, motorbikes, risk-watches, accumulation of."

He appears to be made entirely of gold.

The Angry Nurse leers.

The nice boy trembles, shrinks, backs away sideways out of the IT lounge, and retreats along the corridor, becoming more invisible as he goes, trying his hardest to be nonexistent. Doing his best not to be.

"Do Not Obstruct," says the sign.

My daughter is washing my feet, damn her.

Felicity and Charity are by the window with their smart phones. They are about to begin university. Outside the window is a parking lot. Inside their phones is their future. Are their futures.

"Just forget it, Mom," says my daughter.

"Of course," I tell her. "Certainly. Forget what?"

She sighs.

We have been discussing my son, I think. His investments, the hiccups in his cash flow, his Power of Eternal.

My daughter does not wish to hear about my password, or my urgent need to remember it.

It's not the password that makes her so angry, I think, it's the need.

Which is urgent.

My son with his carefully wiped account. My account, his care. My careful son who comes almost every day to lie to me about money, who writes in the big diary that today we are to have a nice talk about enhanced security alcohols and flexible access options, going forward.

He is not, according to the big diary, going to take me somewhere nice for morning tea. Knowing this makes me look back in the big diary at the last time he did, which appears to have been more recently than the invention of the steam engine, on a Sunday. I think I would quite like to go somewhere nice for morning tea again, if only to see the sea and watch those penguins with their enormous beaks and, hopefully, to witness them swallow someone's Chihuahua.

We are not going anywhere for morning tea today, not only because my son doesn't like doing it, and not only because it isn't written in the diary, but because today, as well as visiting his mother, he must also visit the Scare Manager in his office, which he also hasn't written in the diary. But I know about it anyway, being, as it happens, in the vicinity of the Scare Manager's office with my ear to the door when they are in there discussing extraordinary cash flow entitlements and expeditious access to emergency funds and discrete disbursement of entrepreneurial encirclements via ex-gratia exclusivity enablements. While they discuss these things they admire the growing piles of gold on the Scare Manager's desk, even as more trolleys piled high with laundering and golden turtles are wheeled through the big sliding glass entrance doors, where the Angry Nurse checks them off against her clipboard, unless she happens to be otherwise occupied hitting people on the knee with hammers or roaming the corridors with pillows looking for people who can no longer afford to pay.

"You do trust me, don't you, Mom?" my son says.

"Of course I do, son," I say. "It's written right here in the diary." And I pretend to look for it.

I find this quite enjoyable except that it reminds me of having forgotten that it is right here that the nice boy wrote *forget*. Or *fuck it,* or something. The nice boy whose probational pathway has been problematized. Who has gone to a place where he will not obstruct, where I can only hope he will one day find a toilet that will have him, gone without ever having held me close and been careful with my head the way he did with the fellow who doesn't live here, who also seems to have disappeared, without having managed to find his life, or his password.

But now, of all things, my son goes to the whatsitsname, where I have returned the picture of the older fellow to the back behind the other photos of the Dresser family, and he pushes it toward the front.

"I must go now, Mom," says my son, and although I can't be certain, I think perhaps I hear a hiccup in his cash flow.

"That's all right," I tell him. "I'm expecting the Angry Nurse any minute anyway."

The truth is, what I really need to do is talk to Felicity and Charity about passwords.

Felicity and Chastity listen as I tell them about my password problem. Well, they don't really, of course. They thumb away at their smart phones. My daughter and God aren't listening either, just scrubbing away at my toenails and sighing.

So, since I am certain nobody is listening, I explain everything in some detail, as clearly as I can.

When I am finished, Felicity and Charity are kind enough to stop thumbing and explain to me what it is that I need to do.

"Why don't you just forget it?" says Felicity.

"Forget what?"

My daughter sighs, possibly believing this to be a joke.

"Your account, whatever," says Charity.

Perhaps this is good advice. It seems worth considering. Perhaps I should just forget all about my account. If so, then forgetting my password would seem to be a good start, Shirley. Surely.

"Or," says Felicity. Or Charity. "Just change your password, Granma. Then nobody will know what it is."

"You can change your password?"

You can change? Your password?

"Everything changes, Granma."

"Change is good, Granma."

Well, of course. Still. You can change your past words?

"How?" I say, and I sound just like the older fellow doing his silly impression of a Red Indian from an old movie, when I suggest to him that we might plant some Indian corn, *Zea mays indurata*, or Indian hawthorn, *Rhaphiolepis indica*, or something. This is racist, of course, but it makes me laugh, like it always did. I can't even change that, apparently.

"Go to Settings, Granma."

"Sittings? Like in the dining room? For fish fingers?"

"Settings."

"Of course. Settings. Which is . . . ? Are . . . ?"

"In your account. At the top. Go to the dropdown menu. Then choose Change Details."

Change. Details.

"And to get into my account?" I ask, but I know the answer.

"You'll need your password, Mom," says my daughter, or God. They're enjoying this.

"Simple as that," says Felicity. Or Charity. Their thumbs are a blur. Blurs.

I know what I need. What I need is the nice boy who doesn't mop the floors.

But the nice boy, of course, is nowhere.

The Angry Nurse, however, is everywhere.

The Scare Manager is more and more golden.

The computer in the IT lounge is a mountain.

There are meatballs. There is bingo.

In my window there is a parking lot.
On my door handle there is a piece of silk.
Nevertheless.

There is the noise of the birds. We are in the garden, holding hands.
Not holding, squeezing. And not just the noise of the birds.
As well as the noise of birds, there is the noise of forgetting.
"I forget," he reminds me. "I forget your name."
"Yes," I tell him. "I remember."
At least he laughs.
I do not tell him again that my name is Rose. Instead, I tell
him that I forget too. That I, too, forget.
"Let us . . ." I begin.
"Lettuce," he says. For a moment I hope it might be a joke. Or
that it might be him remembering. But it is just him forgetting.
"Let us forget together," I say.
"That's a good idea," he says. "Us four should get together."
He doesn't laugh.
This makes me happy, since somehow I am sure he means the
four of us. Him and me and my two children. Whom he has never
cared for. For whom he has never cared. Still, I correct him.
"Not us. We. We four."
"Exactly," he says. "The four of us. Whee!"
Then I wonder if perhaps he means the two of us and his
first wife and my first, headless, husband. Shirley not. Surely,
with all this forgetting going on, he doesn't mean we should be
remembering all those earlier, younger, previous, headless people.
But then he squeezes my hand, and I realize he doesn't mean
anything at all.
"There is only us," I tell him, ignoring the noise of the birds.
"There is only you and I. You and me. We will forget together.
Together, we will forget."
We squeeze each other's hand. Hands.

I lie in bed. And that's the truth. Ha-ha. I need to stop making these terrible jokes. They do help the remembering, it's true, though they don't stop the forgetting.

Here I am, in bed. Hanging there on the door handle is a piece of silk, which reminds me that this is not my real, actual bed. It is dark. Not the bed, obviously. That would be racist. Outside the window it is even darker, and there is a parking lot. But also a garden, which is real, as well as actual.

Also real and actual, as far as I can tell, is the Angry Nurse, who stands in the darkness at the end of my bed, where I lie.

The Angry Nurse holds a pillow. That's the truth.

She smiles.

This is unusual. Not the smile. The Angry Nurse in the darkness. Usually it would be the Existentialist girl, checking that my light is out and that my tea things have been taken away, that the piece of silk on my door handle has not been taken away, that my window is shut and that all there is beyond that window is a dark parking lot and not some garden, that the sun has stopped shining and that the birds have stopped making their noise and that I am lying in my bed, not telling the truth but facing up to the ceiling.

But now in the darkness it is the Angry Nurse. She stands close, at the end of the bed, with her pillow. She smiles. Nevertheless, she doesn't appear to be particularly angry.

"I know you are there," I tell her.

"Of course you do, dear," she says.

"I am not afraid," I tell her.

"Of course you aren't," she says.

The pillow is bright in the darkness, like moonlight.

"I have brought you this pillow."

"I don't need your pillow."

"Don't you, dear?"

"I don't want it."

"Really? It's good to have a pillow when you need it."

"You don't scare me."

She smiles some more.

"I am here for you," she says.

It is very, very dark, except for that pillow.

"You have come for me, then?"

"To look after you."

"After me. I wonder. How will you look? After me, I mean."

She smiles. "The same. I will always be the same."

This is a surprise, I must say. Not because it isn't true, but because she says it.

"I am here to scare for you," she says. "That is all I am here for."

"It is very dark through that window," I point out. I want her to know that I know how things are.

"Of course it is," she says.

But she doesn't have any idea. She thinks that through that dark window is just a dark parking lot, an empty dark parking lot without cars and without good sons gently folding their mothers and their walkers into their cars while being careful with their heads and taking them somewhere nice for morning tea even though they hate doing it. And golden motorbikes parked between dark, straight lines, and dead friends with forget-me-nots at their throats, on their backs looking up at the dark sky, and trolleys coming and going through the big dark sliding doors bringing meatballs and laundry and golden turtles.

What she doesn't know is that through that dark window there is also a dark garden, without sunshine and bird noise and without the older fellow and me, I, squeezing each other's hands, and without the names of trees and flowers and vegetables, without terrible jokes about cockatoos and lettuces. Without older fellows, without roses.

"You have no idea," I tell her.

She just looks at me in the light that comes from that pillow.

"What idea don't I have?" she asks me. "What idea, dear?"

It is a reasonable question. She is very good at what she does, this Angry Nurse.

"I forget," I say. For some reason, there seems to be no reason to lie to her. Perhaps it's the pillow. Perhaps I really do want that pillow.

"Remember," she says. Which is easy for her to say. She's not the one who needs a pillow.

"We scare," she says.

This makes me laugh.

"Yeah, sure, whatever," I tell her, just like Felicity and Charity. "You and the Scare Manager. You are both so Person-Centered."

She smiles. Now she is angry, all right. Although, it seems, not at me. She looks at the pillow. It glows in the dark.

"I am here to scare," she says. "That is what I am here for."

"Not to be Holistic?" I say. "Going forward?" It's good to have her angry again. "Not to meet Benchmarks?"

She smiles.

"Even golden ones?" I add. Why should I be nice? She comes in here with a pillow and tells me to remember, and I'm supposed to be careful with her head? As if.

"You might really like this pillow," she says.

I'm tempted, of course. But I have a good son and a busy daughter, and an account and a God who helps clean my toes. I am not nobody.

"I am somebody, you know."

"Is that right, dear?" She squeezes the pillow. So very good at what she does. At least she doesn't call me Rose. I can almost imagine playing Scrabble with her. We would both cheat, of course.

"I have a password."

"Why don't you use it, then?" she says.

She certainly knows how to be surprising.

"I must not obstruct," I point out.

"Obstruct?" she says.

As if she's never seen the word. Even though it's everywhere here, like the opposite of a password. I can't help wandering what the point is to this conversation, what the point is in playing Scrabble when you can't use past words or get past passwords, and how many points there are in the words you can't get past. For that matter, how many points there might be in words that don't exist at all, like Zbtosmty. I'm tired of words. A number of words, anyway. There are words and numbers, numbers and words. Passwords must contain numbers, the fellow who doesn't live here told me when he was trying to find his life inside that mountain in the IT lounge, as usual being the expert about all number of things even though he doesn't even know where he lives.

"It's been nice to chat," I tell the Angry Nurse, who somehow looks more sad than angry. As if there are a number of words she still wants to pass. Words, numbers. Scrabble. Bingo. So many words, and these might be my last, if she has her way with that pillow.

"Enough words," I say. "Take away that pillow. There's a number that need it more than I do. All I need is sleep. Or . . ."

"Or . . . ?" she says, and she's smiling again. It's hard to forget that pillow.

"Or I'll be late for bingo."

She just looks at me.

"Be very, very careful," she says.

I have been searching back through the secret parts of the big diary, looking at the secret things I have written there, as well as the mysterious spaces where pages have been removed.

Here, for example, is the page where the Angry Nurse came for her nighttime visit.

It helps me, I think, to look again at some of the surprising things that happen. To sort out what may really have happened and what may have not. To make sense of things, if not exactly understand them.

Even if I don't find anything, even if the page has been torn out, perhaps even by me, it seems to help me think.

What I am looking for is the night, not long after the visit of the Angry Nurse, that the Scare Manager also came to me in my room. It may have been the same night, for all I know.

This time it's the Mephisphelelean girl who takes away my tea things and turns out the light and checks that the window is closed. And then opens it.

And suddenly the Scare Manager is there in the darkness at

the end of my bed, entirely made of gold. As if he has flown straight in that window from the parking lot on golden wings.

"Rose!" he says in that amazed way he has, as if he has just discovered the name or has made it up himself, instead of me.

"Rose is past tense," I say. "Call me Rise. And shut that window behind you."

"Let's talk about that window," he says.

"It's a parking lot," I remind him.

"You can have any window you want," his voice says from his high, golden head.

"All this could be mine, you mean? Holistically?"

He looks at me. We understand each other.

"Let's talk about your account," he says.

"Let's do that," I say.

But it's him who does the talking. He. He talks about Duty of Scare, of course, and Best Practice and so on, and then he talks about how I can have whatever I want. Whatever window I want, whatever garden I want in that window, whatever bed I want to lie in while I look through that window, whatever room I want that bed to be in, whatever piece of silk I want to be tied to the door handle.

I can have it all, he tells me.

All I have to do is not obstruct.

Naturally, I look at his head as he tells me these things. His golden head high above his golden neck. I can't help being reminded of my first husband, whom I don't remember, except for his head and the way it rose so high above his mighty neck as he told me things, high above me like a mountain telling me things until suddenly, with one stroke, he stopped and became my headless ex-husband, whose head I removed but who continued to manipulate the toes of my children.

There are certain things, the Scare Manager tells me, that I should not look into.

"Like mountains?" I say. And I think of the fellow who doesn't live here, sitting in front of that computer in the IT lounge, looking into that mountain, failing to find his life.

"Your account," he says.

"I'm a cunt?" I say, looking surprised. I might as well have some fun.

"Your account," the Scare Manager says. "Your son . . ."

"He's a good boy. He has a thoroughly wiped bottom. It gleams. Not unlike your head."

"He has access . . ."

"I don't know anything about axes, but he does have the Power of Eternal."

It's funny. The Scare Manager looks around the room just the way my son does. They are quite alike in some ways.

"It's all about access to available funds," he says. "Responding flexibly to changing needs, going forward."

"Of course," I say. "It's about cash flow and hiccups, and golden turtles and Benchmarks, and it's about always having to pay more."

This is not going the way he expected, I expect.

"And it's about lying to me about money, it's about transition-ing me if I don't keep paying more, it's about my son knowing my password and using it to cure his hiccups and to pay for your golden turtles and risk-watches, and it's about selling my window to anyone who can pay more than I can."

"Rose, it is about Individual Person-Centered Scare. It's about—"

"Speaking of which, the Individual with the nasty lines on his neck, whose son was driven away by the police so that he couldn't keep paying more, ended up with his own Individual pillow. Not to mention my friend with the forget-me-nots around her neck who ended up Individually on her back in the parking lot, which is what I see now when I look out my window. . . ."

This gets him excited, and his golden head gets goldener, his neck gets neckier.

"You can have any window you want, Rose."

"What I want is a nice game of Scrabble with my friend."

"Rose, your son—"

"In fact, let's have a game now. You and me. Hand me that

board. You'll like it. It's fun to cheat. What color would you like? Gold, of course. I'll take black. And white."

"Your son has mentioned some confusion about passwords . . ."

"Yes, he does seem confused at times. I'll start. Five-letter word. Fraud. Like Sigmund Fraud the doctor, or whatever he was. Now your turn. How about Embezzlement? Or Beelzebub? Better still, Embeelzebubment. My turn. Pass that board to me so I can make a word. A password. I know, I'll use my own password. Now, what is it again? Zbtosmty? No, that's not right. Let me think. . . . It'll come to me. I bet you know it anyway. My password is . . ."

But he's too cunning to be tricked that way, the golden devil. He says nothing. Which is unusual enough in itself. Then I realize something. He's waiting. And he's excited. So high and golden and yet so excited about what silly thing I might say next that he looks like he might be about to leave a big golden Benchmark all over the Scrabble board. So high above me with his golden head on his golden neck, but suddenly so silent that he reminds me of my first husband at the exact moment that *he* suddenly went silent, when he was struck by his stroke and became my headless ex–first husband. And I am struck now myself, by this excited Scare Manager who waits in silence so high above me. Waiting for me, because I am very old and very stupid, to tell him my password. Because he doesn't know what it is. He doesn't have a clue. Suddenly I know that he doesn't know any more than I do.

Because my son.

Because my good, loving son.

Because my good, loving son with his thoroughly wiped bottom and his cash flow hiccups hasn't told him.

"You don't know, do you?" I say.

"What?" is all he can say, for all his gold.

"What it is."

"What is it?" he says.

"Exactly," I say.

"Rose," he says, "I don't know—"

"No, you don't, do you? You don't know my password. And you don't know it because my son has refused to tell you."

My son. My dear, good, loving son. My son who comes every day and steals from my account and lies to me for the sake of his own cash flow hiccups and to help the Scare Manager meet his golden Benchmarks, going forward, but who has never told the Scare Manager his poor old mother's password, whatever it might be. My poor, dear, loving son. Who loves his mother so much that he has assumed the full reprehensibility, responsibility, of lying to her and stealing from her account. So that whenever the Scare Manager needs to reach new golden Benchmarks, he must go helmet in hand to my good son and threaten him with his mother losing her window or being thrown out of it, or else being smothered in the middle of the night with her own Individual, Person-Centered pillow. What a good, loving son he is, to have taken upon himself all this freud, fraud and embeelzebubment, just as my good, loving daughter takes upon herself the task of putting my potted plants in the bathtub and washing my toes with nobody to help her but her busy, resentful God.

"Your son and your daughter love you very much," the Scare Manager says, reading my mind.

Never has he reminded me more of my headless husband. Never has he reminded me less of the older fellow in the garden, who had no gold but did have the most beautiful neck, even if he never loved my children.

"You will never know my password," I tell him.

"You never know," he says.

He is very close to killing me now, I suspect.

"I am about to change it," I say. "And then nobody will know it."

I say this with my best Scrabble face on.

"Don't forget . . ." he begins, and I almost laugh.

"Of course I'll forget," I say. "That's what I do."

He's not listening. He leans forward and is very close to me now. He gleams in the darkness. Behind him is the parking lot in my window. In which I will soon be on my back staring at the sky, forget-me-nots or not.

"Don't forget," he says again. "Don't forget your son. Don't forget your daughter."

"They are good children," I say.

He is growing larger, and I am getting smaller.

"Bad things can happen to good children," he says.

He is like a mountain of gold.

"What do you mean?" I say, but I know what he means.

"Going forward," he says.

I try to imagine my life without the big diary, without the picture of the older fellow being moved to the front of the whatsitsname, without being taken somewhere nice for morning tea, without my potted plants being watered, without my bathtub being scrubbed, without a piece of silk on my doorknob. It's Holistic.

The Scare Manager smiles. He has said enough, and he knows it. He doesn't leave by the window. He is so big by now that he can barely make it through the door.

And in his place is the Angry Nurse again, with that pillow. Where did she come from?

She grins at me. It is terrible.

"Are you absolutely certain that you don't need this pillow?" she says.

The big diary lies open on the whatsitsname, beside the photos of the Dresser family.

The nice boy wrote *forget*. But I can't forget, any more than I can remember.

The diary is open at tomorrow.

Nothing is written on the page.

My son is a good son. It is possible that I have never wanted more than I do now to see that he intends to take me somewhere nice for morning tea.

But it is something more that I need, from someone else.

I turn more pages. I go past tomorrow, into the future.

Every one of the pages is . . . what do you call it. Blank.

I need to find a new place in the diary. An empty, private place I have never found before.

I go to the very last page.

At the bottom of this final page, I write. What I write, I write very small and sort of sideways, so that it is hardly there at all, hidden away in its secret corner so that I know it will be found.

But only by the nice boy.

Help me, please.

The older fellow squeezes my hand. We are in the garden, sitting side by side on the whatsitsname, surrounded by sunshine, bird noise, roses.

"I forget," he says.

"It's Rose."

"Of course," he says. "Yes."

I don't ask him what *his* name is.

"Let us forget together," I say.

"Lettuce," he says, possibly. I'm hoping for one of his jokes.

"It won't be long," I say.

"It isn't very long now," he says. "It never was very long, really." This, perhaps, is a joke, but there is no laughter.

I squeeze his hand.

"It's on the way."

"Yes. Of course it is."

"Here it is now."

"There it is. Now."

Because through the open gate we can both see the whatsit

arriving. The ambulance. It is yellow and it gleams, like gold. I
have stopped thinking about the older fellow's neck. Those spots
that I loved so much. And my children, whom he did not love. I
begin to remember my children.

"It's time," I say.

"Yes," he says. "That's what it is, all right."

He has no idea what I'm talking about.

The ambulance rehearses toward us. Reverses. It makes its
ugly beeping noise, nothing at all like the noise of birds.

I watch as they put him in. They don't need to put him on
a . . . trolley, for delivering. A what do you call it, stretcher, for
stretching. A bed, for lying. They allow him to sit up in front,
like a child going for a ride to somewhere nice. As they help
him into the gleaming ambulance, they are careful with his
head.

"Let us," he says from the window.

"Lettuce what?" I ask, still hoping for a joke.

"Forget."

"Yes," I tell him. "Together."

"We two," he says.

"We too," I say.

But instead of forgetting, I remember. I remember that first
day, when I first came through this gate, into this garden with its
roses and its noise of birds, and how a laughing whatsitsname, lunatic, flew straight at my head like some sort of lorikeet. Not
being careful with my head at all. Making me duck, like some
sort of duck. Flying right through the space where my head was.
Perhaps it's still there. Not still, but there. Not my head, but the
lunatic.

I remember that day how it made the older fellow laugh, like
a lorikeet.

And now I remember this final day, watching them drive him
away, being very, very careful with his head.

I try to be careful with my own.

It's no use.

"I love you," I say.
And suddenly, all around me is the noise of birds.
Trichoglossus moluccanus.
Callocephalon fimbriatum.
Laughing, like lunatics.

I am so tired. Not that I can sleep. I lie in bed with Somalia. Insomnia. Perhaps I need to face up to things. Apart from the ceiling.

Perhaps I should give up.

Perhaps I should let go.

Perhaps that is what the nice boy meant when he wrote *forget*.

Perhaps I should make it easier for myself, and for everyone else.

Perhaps it would be better if I were dead.

I would miss the meatballs, obviously. But at least it wouldn't go on forever, like these nights in Somalia.

Perhaps it is not so bad, being dead.

I will ask my friend.

I get out of bed and go looking for her.

"Zbtosmty," she says, which is typical of her, and no help at all. Anyway, she is busy falling out of windows.

So I go wondering with my walker along the empty corridors, until I find myself once more in the IT lounge.

The computer is dark, but it lights up when I touch the piano. The mountain appears.

I sit in front of that mountain for a long time. Nothing happens. The mountain continues to be a mountain. It is certainly inspirational, but not much more interesting than the ceiling.

So I go over to the pile of old encephalograms, encyclopedias, in the corner and amuse myself for a while. I look up things about mountains. Not new mountains such as you might find on a computer but old ones from the Bible. There is Mount Sinai, where Moses got the Twelve Commandments, and Mount Arrowroot, where Noah's ark washed up. Also another mountain, where Jesus had an interesting conversation with Satan. Satan may not really have been there, according to some experts, but you have to remember that Jesus had been wondering for forty days and forty nights in the whatsitsname, without so much as a biscuit.

Even though these stories are more interesting than looking at the ceiling, they're not getting me anywhere. Or not where I want to get, wherever that is. So I turn off the light and leave the IT lounge and wonder along the corridor some more until I reach the revelator and, beside it, the door to the Fiery Escape stairs. I open the door, with some difficulty, and keep it open with my walker. The stairs are dark, and although there is no sign of the fire at the bottom, I know it must be there far below, and that down there somewhere also is the secret place where the drugs are bought and sold as well as the pizzas, and the little children are murdered by the lizard people. According to my friend, anyway, and she would know.

Just as she knew how easily a person might be thrown down these stairs and have their neck broken.

I wish my friend were here now. Because now, standing at the top of these fiery stairs thinking about my neck getting broken, I feel something all around me. A glow, all around me, glowing. At first I think it must be from the fire.

But it isn't a fiery glow, or not entirely.

It is a golden glow.

The Scare Manager.

I feel his power. I feel it behind me, above me, crowding in on me, all over me.

In front of me, before me, below me, the stairs are stairier, steeper, deeper, neck-breakier.

"Rose," he says.

He sounds different. I don't like it.

"You're a long way from where you should be, Rose."

He doesn't even pretend to be nice. It's a while since he bothered to make one of those unfunny jokes of his about how good I look and how the fellows need to watch out. But I don't look good, I know that. I haven't had any sleep for forty days and forty nights and I am still, I'm ashamed to say, in my nightgown. It would almost be nice to hear him trying out his bedside manners and going on about everything being Holistic and Person-Centered, going forward. But he doesn't bother with all that either. There's nobody here to hear him.

There appears to be no way out but down those stairs. And it's a long, long way down, down to where the fire is.

I don't want to turn to look at him. It is bad enough that he is there, and that I knew he would be.

But I do turn, and there he is.

He smiles, like a shark with a beach ball.

So. This is it. After all this time, it is time.

"I know what you are going to do," I say.

And I wait for him to do it.

And continue waiting.

"I'm not going to do anything," he says.

"You're not going to push me down these stairs, break my neck?"

"I don't need to, Rose. Do I?"

He's smarter than I thought.

"It's a long way down. And you are not very steady on your feet, are you, Rose? If you were to just let go of that walker, and lean forward a little, you might very easily overbalance. And topple."

"Topple?" It's a funny word. Although not so funny that I should laugh, but I do. Or giggle, at least. It must be nervousness, or excitement, or the fact that it's the middle of the night and I'm standing at the top of a stairway that is so high you can't even see the fire at the bottom, and am in my nightgown having a conversation with a powerful force that might not even be there.

"It would all be over very quickly," he says.

"You might not even be here," I tell him.

"You either," he says.

Oh dear. He knows what I am afraid of.

"You might already be dead, Rose. You know that, don't you?"

"I'm not really sure I know anything."

Oh dear. Now I'm telling him the truth. That's not like me at all. Perhaps I'm asleep.

"You could easily find out, once and for all. Just lean forward a little. Just let go. That's all you need to do. And then you'll know for certain. Either you'll be dead, and it will all be over, or else you're already dead, but at least you'll know for certain."

I am tempted.

I take my hand off the walker. I lean forward. The more I lean, the higher the stairs become. It is like being at the top of a very high mountain. I see almost to the bottom, where the fire must be, and I see myself toppling. I see myself breaking my neck. I see the Scare Manager behind me, smiling his golden smile.

I lean forward a little more.

And then I laugh. Which must be from all the excitement. But also that all this thinking about mountains and necks makes me think some more about mountains and necks.

About my headless first husband with his mighty neck that I looked up to, and how as I looked up, he lost his head with one stroke and toppled, like a mountain.

And about the older fellow, and how lovely those spots of his were because they were not something else and we could go on holding hands in that garden in the sunshine forever.

The laughter comes from deep in my belly, like a bellow, or a bellows. It might even put the fire out. Put out the fire. Or else make it worse.

"Stop laughing," says the Scare Manager.

He's right, of course. Because, of course, there was something the older fellow had forgotten.

I stop laughing.

"Just a little more," he says, behind me. "Just let yourself go a little more, and it will all be over."

Again I see the older fellow being driven away, out of the garden.

I teeter.

I even totter.

But I don't topple.

Behind me, the Scare Manager is becoming quite annoyed.

"Go on," he says. "You know you want to."

He's right. He is very good at what he does. It is, perhaps, what I want. Or it is time for it, at least.

But then there is something. Something that is almost here. Something I can almost hear.

"This is no life, Rose. You don't want to go on living like this, surely?"

I can't help myself. I start laughing again. I can't stop. Because I really can hear something. We are nowhere near a window, but there is light. There is daylight, there is sunshine, somewhere. Soon it will be everywhere. I know this because I hear it coming. It is the very faint sound of a very loud noise, far away and coming closer.

The noise of birds, flying right at me.

"I don't know if it's a life or not, but whatever it is . . ."

And I turn around to face him, but he is not there, so I don't bother.

I really do have to laugh.

"And don't call me Shirley."

My walker and I get moving again. We make our way back along the brightening corridors. The noise of the birds is very loud now and becomes mixed up with all the usual morning sounds of this place. Of cups of tea and medications and knees being hit with tiny hammers and meatballs and bingo.

I pass one "Do Not Obstruct" sign after another.

I know what it is that I must do.

I am thinking about the nice boy who no longer mops the floors.

And I am thinking about obstructing.

Here I am in my room.

I know what it is that I will do. I will make something happen.

Nothing happens.

Here I am lying in my bed, facing up to the ceiling. It is just another night. And it seems like it might go on forever, like all the other nights.

Except that now I know better. I know that things never change, until they do. Nothing ever happens, and then it happens very quickly.

Nothing happens for a bit longer.

Then the nice boy comes out of my bathroom, with his mop.

Or perhaps not. Not that it isn't the nice boy, which it is, and not that it isn't my bathroom that he comes out of, which it is. It's the mop that I'm not so sure of. Let's say that he does have his mop, because that's the way I like to imagine it, and also because it might explain what he's been doing in my bathroom. Unless he's discovered that it's a trans-friendly bathroom, which I'd like to think it is, although I can't be certain.

Anyway, it is the nice boy, and it's lovely to see him. If he's not exactly mopping the floor, he is certainly moving sideways, or uncertainly moving sideways, if not backward. Advancing and at the same time what do you call it—retweeting. Drawing and withdrawing. Appearing and disappearing behind his curtain of fringe, his earrings glimmering in his eyebrows and his nose and his lips and even, it seems, his tongue, although that can't be right. And his breasts, which somehow seem bigger than ever.

"Come closer," I tell him. "Let me see that amazing bosom of yours."

This is possibly the wrong thing to say, since he moves away backward and sideways and says something from behind his fringe which might be "*get fucked*" or "*fuck off*" or "*motherfucker*," but as usual he swallows the words as he says them, and the only way I know that he wants to come closer is that he moves farther away.

"I've been thinking," I say, which isn't exactly true. Feeling, imagining, wondering. Remembering, possibly, although I forget.

"I think I might know what my password is."

"Fuck it," the nice boy says, and slides away toward the corner of the room, turning his back toward me instead of his bosom.

I have his attention.

He won't come closer while I'm lying in bed, so I do the only thing I can, which is stop lying and get out of bed. I don't want to use my walker, but my legs have other ideas, so I sort of lurch sideways at the nice boy, who of course lurches sideways himself, and before we know it we're lurching sideways together around the room, with me hanging on to him as if he's my savior, or my mop, so that if anyone saw the two of us it would look like we were what do you call it, waltzing, very badly, in the darkness.

"Fuck it, fuck it, fuck it," the nice boy whispers into my ear, I think.

"I know, I know, I know," I say.

We are so close. I hang on to him for dear life.

"My darling," I say. I can't help myself.

He is so nice, he says nothing.

So we what do you call it around the room for a while longer. He is so gentle with me, and holds me so close, while all the time he's trying to get away from me.

"I need your help," I tell him.

"Fuck off," he says, and I know everything will be all right.

Eventually, by continuing to go in the wrong direction, we get to where I want us to go, which is to the door. He tries very gently to push me away, but I push back and so we continue sideways and backward, out into the corridor. And we continue, waltzing together along the corridors, past the "Do Not Obstruct" signs, one step forward and two steps somewhere else, until we arrive, somehow, at the IT lounge.

This may not be exactly how it happens, but it does happen, and it is how I remember it, so whatever.

Someone else is already there in the IT lounge.

It is the fellow who doesn't live here, sitting alone in the darkness in front of the computer, looking at the mountain. He looks as if he has been there a long time. He looks as if he has given up on waiting for something to happen. He looks as if he hasn't any strength left to move that mountain.

Though he does brighten when he sees us, or at least when he sees the nice boy. As if he knows as well as I do that the nice boy is our only chance.

He makes room for us in front of the computer, and watches over my shoulder as we get started. Or as the nice boy gets started, and I watch over the nice boy's shoulder.

We look at the mountain.

The nice boy touches the piano, and the mountain disappears. Simple as that. But in its place is a slot, like a letterbox. Even this is no problem for the nice boy. So many things are, but not this.

"Cunt," he says. Or "Code," possibly, and puts it in. This makes a little line of Tintins, Asterixes, appear in the letterbox, which then disappears.

And then we set about doing the opposite of forgetting together.

It doesn't even take all that long, thanks to the nice boy. He knows, or guesses, the name of the bank where my account lives. Perhaps he even knows *my* name. I don't ask.

But now my username. Apparently I have one.

He waits. Waiting is not a problem for him. Not for me either, really, it just takes a while.

And a while more.

Then.

"I am not Rose," I say. And all he does is type it in. As if he is not surprised at all. The nice boy is many things, but surprised is not one of them.

But it isn't right.

The nice boy waits.

I am. I am not. I am what I am. And then the older fellow in the garden with his silly jokes about vegetables. I yam what I yam.

"I yam not Rose."

The nice boy puts it in. Takes away the spaces. No good. Adds a number one. Still no good. Tries a different one. Not one, another number altogether. Two.

Bingo. It's correct.

But now my password.

The nice boy waits. We can do this. You can do this. We can do this together. All these things he does not say. We are very close.

"Try zbtosmty," I tell him. This is almost fun.

But no.

It is the older fellow in the garden. Of course it is.

"I love you," I say.

The nice boy doesn't even try it.

"Fuck it," he says.

"You've said that before, I recall."

And I also recall him writing it in the big diary. So that I could see the words, not just hear the muffled, sideways sound of him swallowing them down as he speaks.

"Forget."

And I see, one more time, the older fellow in the garden.

"Forget together."

The nice boy and I are so close. I might even squeeze his hand.

"Let us forget together," I say.

He puts it in. It's not right. I almost laugh.

"Lettuce," I say.

"Fuck it together," he says.

"Exactly. Lettuce forget together."

"Bum pervs," mumbles the nice boy. Numbers.

"Lettuce four get together."

He puts it in. Then he takes away all the space.

Lettuce4get2gether.

Bingo.

At last, my account. Here I am inside it, and I can see everything. It is all here.

It is extremely boring.

Never the less. There is always more. And the more we look, the more we see. As well as lots of little lies put there by my son, little fiddlings to fix his cash flow hiccups, there are much bigger lies and much larger numbers that pass through my account. Coming from somewhere and going somewhere else and made to look like something different along the way, like laundry. Money from the poor souls in this place who have been transitioned because they could not pay more, and even more money from those who could. All of it hiding there in the darkness of my account, well away from any light, before flowing on down secret corridors to meet the Scare Manager's Benchmarks, going forward.

I can't say I understand it, and yet it all makes sense.

"Motherfucker," the nice boy says.

Exactly.

The fellow who doesn't live here becomes quite animalistic, animated, over my shoulder.

"The bastards!" he says.

"Shush," I tell him. I don't like it when he swears.

The fellow who doesn't live here understands it all, apparently, the way he does. He starts explaining everything in detail, so that it becomes even more boring. I think he's quite impressed. Everything is so thorough, everything is so organized, everything is so detailed. And it's all lies. All zbtosmty. All cheating at Scrabble. All smiling sharks.

My account is the hidden center of things, where change happens. Transactions, transitions, transformations. Everything changing, everything turning into something different, and all of it turning into piles of gold on the Scare Manager's desk.

Change is good, of course. So I make a few. I transition. With the nice boy's help, I make some trans actions of my own. He does the actual piano-playing, of course. And the fellow who doesn't live here becomes more and more excited over my shoulder, offering advice and making his own suggestions, as if he understands everything about everything. It is lovely to see him so happy.

I make my account my own again. I make changes, on my own account. I untie bits of silk and reattach them in different ways in different places to different door handles. I can change the direction of things, it seems. I can change how things flow. So I do. Or the nice boy does. The nice boy knows about changes.

I have no idea what I'm doing, but I do it thoroughly, fearlessly, and without mercy.

There is one thing I know for certain. I know that whatever will happen as a result, it would not have happened without me.

When we are finished, there is one more thing to do. The biggest thing, perhaps. I remember what Felicity and Charity told me, about the step they said was so simple and would make my account once more my very own, my personal, my secret thing.

I go into Settings.

And I change my password.

Oh dear, what excitement I have caused.

Not to mention confusion, astonishment, bewilderment, disruption, and dismay.

It is very enjoyable indeed.

The Scare Manager is locked in his office with my son and the Angry Nurse. As I happen to be wandering past with my ear pressed against the door, I hear the Scare Manager threatening my son, which is not pleasant, and yelling at the Angry Nurse, which is. My son seems to have a particularly bad case of the hiccups. The Angry Nurse is speaking very softly, which is never good. She may even be smiling. The Scare Manager sounds not only furious but also frightened, which is the pleasantest thing of all.

When my son comes to see me in my room, he looks for a long time at the door handle, as if he's lost. I tell him not to worry, that it really is me. Then I read out to him what is written in the big diary: "I have a new password."

He can't even manage to look around the room the way he usually does, the poor dear. Being able to access my account has been very important to him.

"Change is good," I remind him.

My darling son. He can't even look at me. He has a dirty bottom. He is so ashamed. If only he had God, like his sister does. My daughter who is never ashamed, only tired and angry. Perhaps I should invite him into my bathroom, so he can kneel down and put his head on the edge of the bathtub.

It's all right, I tell him, it's all right. He still has the Power of Eternal. He will always have that. Trust me. And I don't mind about his cash flow; he can help himself whenever he has the hiccups. It's only the Scare Manager's gold that I don't want flowing through my account, all those turtles leaving their nasty Benchmarks everywhere, all those people falling out of windows because they can't pay more, all those dead old men lying in my bed with their mouths open.

I tell him it's all all right. I tell him it's the Scare Manager, not him. I tell him that all I want is to have the Scare Manager's Benchmarks scrubbed clean like a bathtub. Then he can steal all the cash from me he needs to deal with his hiccups, and he can lie to me as much as he likes and he can have the Power of Eternal forever.

I tell him that he mustn't worry, that I will tell him my new password, of course I will.

Soon.

My daughter sighs. She is kneeling beside the bathtub with God. Felicity and Chastity are by the window with their thumbs and their smart phones.

"Mom," my daughter says. "Your password . . ."

So, she has been speaking to her brother. It's nice to think that the two of them sometimes get together and speak about their mother.

"It's all right," I tell her. "I'll tell your brother what my new password is. Of course I will. But not just yet. There is something I want to happen first."

"Mom," she says, then she gives up and rests her head on the edge of the bathtub.

"Stop talking to God for a minute," I tell her. "This is what I want. I want you and your brother to come and see me together, here in this room, at the same time."

This surprises her.

"We need to talk," I say.

This surprises her even more.

The nice boy has vanished again, but I don't let this worry me. I know that he disappears, and that he returns. I know that he will not abandon me. And I know that I will not abandon him.

The nice boy has done so much for me. The last thing he did for me, the last time I saw him, was in the IT lounge when we made all the changes.

I let him choose my new password. It seemed like the least I could do.

It is a lovely password. I am so glad to have it. It makes me very happy. And it makes other people nervous and frightened, which is particularly satisfying.

I love my new password.

But. Except.

There's just one problem.

I forget what it is.

I am lying in bed again. It is the middle of the night again. Well, to be truthful, I have no idea what time of the night it is. I am reasonably certain that I am not asleep. And although I am in bed, I am not lying. Trust me.

Although I am in bed, I have decided not to lie.

My children are here. My son and my daughter, together. I have summoned them, and here they are. They stand beside the bed looking concerned.

Apparently, I have not been well. Some medication issues, they tell me. Personally, I wouldn't be surprised if it was poison, although I'm no expert.

"You haven't been well," my daughter tells me.

"I haven't been all sorts of things. That's what I want to talk to you about."

The more I think about it, the more I think it must be close to the end of what has been a very long night. Just before morning. Whatever. The end of something. The beginning of something else.

There is something else unusual about these children of mine, apart from their being here together by my bedside before dawn. As far as I can tell, they are both about ten years old.

My son appears to be sulking, which is understandable since he is a liar and a thief, and my daughter has that look of hers that says everybody lies and thieves, except her, obviously, since she has God and is very, very tired, even if she is only ten years old.

But I have a surprise for them. A number of surprises, really.

The first surprise is that in bed with me is their father, my headless first husband.

I show them the photo. I have been hiding it under the bed-clothes. They look even more concerned, and even more as if they are ten years old. Ten years old with a dead father.

They even begin to cry.

Stop that, I want to tell them. Shit happens.

But I don't, because I intend not only to tell the truth but to be nice. And possibly they are crying not just because their father has no head, but because I have gone to the trouble of putting the photo in a nice new frame. You can hardly even see the tear across the top.

"I understand," I say. "I understand that you loved him."

This surprises them so much that they cry some more.

"I understand how much I hurt you."

They keep crying.

"And I have always understood your need for revenge."

This stops the crying. They look at me all confused and inno-cent, as if they don't understand me, since they are only children. They don't fool me for a second.

I tell them that I know they loved their father, and that he loved them, and that possibly he even loved me, although that seems unlikely. And that after the stroke that struck his head from his mighty neck, they felt betrayed and abandoned by their mother going off with another fellow and being loved in a garden.

I don't go into the whole . . . choreography, chronology, of this. I don't point out that the fellow who loved me in a garden

was a much older fellow, and that I am reasonably certain my
children were no longer ten years old when it happened.

"I do understand that you never really stop being children
when it comes to your feelings. We are all children. None of us
ever really grow up. I understand that. Pain and hurt and be-
trayal and abandonment always remain the same age. As does
love, I suppose."

Still, get over it, is what I would say if I had not decided to be
nice as well as truthful.

"None of us grow up, we just grow older," I tell them. "Just
look at me."

But they don't look at me. I don't blame them. It is not about
me. Except of course in all the ways that it is.

This is not going so well. My son and my daughter stand
there on either side of my bed looking ten, and waiting. I know
exactly what they are waiting for. I know what they have always
been waiting for. I know exactly what they want me to say.

"I am sorry," I say. "I really am sorry."

And it does seem to make them a little happier to hear me say
this. Perhaps they even believe it. As if I would be sorry for going
away to a garden and being loved and having my head filled with
bird noise and laughter. But I must try harder.

"I am obviously a bad mother."

This goes down a treat. Because they are ten, they don't even
pretend to disagree.

"But what can I tell you?" I say. "I lost my head." And because their father is here beside me in bed as I say this, I start
laughing.

Nothing. They never get the joke, these kids of mine.

I need to try harder.

I must forget. I must encourage them to forget. Encourage.
Fill with courage. Let us have the courage to forget together.

I tell them again that I understand. That I understand that
when their mother went off with an older fellow who didn't care
about them and who never tickled their toes and who only cared

about loving their bad mother and growing his vegetables and making his terrible jokes, they kept on being ten years old. And that they remained ten years old even after they discovered the things they were good at and how these things might help them pass in the world for grown-ups. How my son learned to clean his bottom so thoroughly, scrubbing away at it until the cash flowed, and how my daughter learned so well how to do the thing that her bad mother never did, which was sacrifice herself for others, or for God or Jesus or whatever.

"You have both done so well," I tell them. "I am very proud of you."

They look partly pleased at this, and partly nervous.

"Of course, it has been important to you to remain unhappy. And you have both been very good at that. You have really worked hard at it. You have both brought up happy children while always taking great care not to be happy yourselves."

They certainly don't look happy now, although they do appear pleased to be praised for their efforts.

"Let me tell you, you have succeeded. You have been most effective in demonstrating to your mother how she should have gone about bringing up her own children to be happy while avoiding, at all costs, her own happiness."

My son looks as though he would much prefer me to talk about how he has been emaciating, embroidering, embezzling my account, as well as helping the Scare Manager with his laundry and his piling up of gold Benchmarks through the clever reassignment of bits of silk to various door handles.

My daughter looks as if she would much prefer this also, so she could then exercise her hard-won, ten-year-old's wisdom to counsel tolerance of her brother as the flawed character he is, and offer to put in a good word for him with God before getting on with the business of carrying another armful of potted plants into my bathroom.

Oh, no you don't. If there's any understanding going to be done here, I'm the one who's going to be doing it.

"I understand, my son, that you have tried your best to become your father. And I understand, my daughter, that you have tried very hard to be the opposite of your mother."

They don't look at me. They don't look at each other. I wave the photo of my headless husband at them, and they look at that instead.

"Let us four get together," I say. "It's about time."

They look confused, which of course is enjoyable, but nevertheless. I must make sense.

"Let us forget together."

Which is my password, of course. Or was, until I remembered it. Because then, of course, I had to change it. And then I had a beautiful new password, which was all my own. But then, of course, I forgot it.

So here we are. Forgetting. Together.

Even so, that isn't all we need to do.

"Get me that big diary from on top of the whatsitsname."

And I read to them what I have found there, written very small and beautifully in a secret corner of the final page so that it could only have been put there by the nice boy, because he had not forgotten. Because I needed his help and he knew that this was the help I needed.

My new password.

It doesn't look much. It looks a lot like *give a fuck*, but only because the nice boy gets everything back to front and sideways as well as having trouble with his bowels. Vowels.

Forgive, is what it says.

Let us forgive, together.

It is my new password. And now I tell it to my son, and to my daughter.

"I have decided to allow you to forgive me," I say. But I must be nice.

"And I forgive you too."

Lettuce4give2gether.

Bingo.

"But first," I tell them, "this is what is going to happen."

From now on, I tell them, they will both have the Power of Eternal. It was wrong of me—as well as racist, I now understand—to give only my son the Power of Eternal, just because he was so much like his father. Now my daughter will have it equally, and forever. Or until.

And then when the time comes, of course, they will both be my executioners. I know they will do a good job.

First, though, there will be change. And change is good, I remind them. First, they will help me to tell the truth about this place. About accounts and laundries and bits of silk on door handles and people falling out of windows. About the Scare Manager and his golden Benchmarks.

Speaking of change, it seems that my children have stopped being ten years old, which is something of a relief. Perhaps my medication issues have corrected themselves.

I point at the TV high up in the corner.

"I want to see the truth up there on that TV," I tell them. "I want to see people up there sitting side by side behind coffee cups, agreeing with each other about what the truth is."

My son looks confused, then looks very brave and serious and grown-up, as if he's been waiting for this, and says something about his responsibility, and about becoming a whistleblower. This makes my daughter look annoyed, as if she smells sacrilege, sacrifice, and has no intention of allowing her brother to be the only one to do the sacrificing. But I tell them we will all blow the whistle together. We will all have whistles, and we will blow them all. I'm not entirely sure why we're suddenly talking about whistles, which seems a bit childish, but then I remember that until very recently they have been ten years old.

"We will all be whistlers," I say. "We will be *Pachycephala pectoralis*."

They look at me.

"Golden whistler. It's a bird."

And right then the light arrives. The light of day coming in, the sunlight, through the parking lot and into the window. We all see the light, but the best of it is what can't be seen. The sound.

The noise. The birds. The calling, the singing, the chattering and warbling and screeching and trilling, the tweeting and retweeting and laughing and loving. And, perhaps, the golden whistling.

"Can you hear that?" I ask my children.

"Hear what?" they say.

The poor dears.

N othing happens.
      Then things happen very quickly.
      "Look, Granma, something's happening!" says Felicity.
      "Look, Granma, look!" says Charity.
      It's lovely to see them so excited.
      It's something very important, and it is happening, although where it is happening is hard to say. Out the window, in the parking lot, on the TV hanging high in the corner, possibly even on Felicity's and Chastity's smart phones, or possibly all these places at once. And it is happening now, or perhaps yesterday, or else tomorrow, whatever.
      But it is happening, I am reasonably confident of that.
      My daughter has come out of the bathroom to look. Even God seems to have come out with her, although obviously I can't be certain.
      We all look at the TV. Or the window. Felicity and Chastity look at their smart phones.
      What we see is the parking lot. And cars arriving in the

parking lot. Police cars. Filled with police. Police who look like police as well as police who don't look like police, but all police. And the big glass entrance doors sliding open, and the police going through that entrance as if there is nothing that can stop them, whether they look like police or not. And there are others who aren't police but are pointing cameras and whatsits, microscopes, microphones. All of them being very excited by the entrance, as if they are entranced. And now police coming out again, carrying boxes and computers and pianos and Scrabble boards and trolleys piled high with more boxes filled with papers and files and folders and, I can only assume, meatballs and laundry.

"Someone's in deep shit," says Felicity.

"Someone's totally fucked," says Charity.

"It's Holistic," I tell them.

"Jesus, what have we done?" my daughter asks. Retroactively, I assume. Rhetorically.

Jesus, or God, or whatever his name is, doesn't say anything.

Things are certainly changing. Nothing ever changes, then it does, very quickly indeed. And it's Person-Centered.

"You did this, Mom!" says my daughter. "You made it happen!"

She wants me to feel guilty, of course. She can't help herself.

"Change is good," I tell her, and I'm already halfway out the door with my walker. I am not going to miss out on this. It's been a long time since I, or my walker, moved this fast.

"Way to go, Granma!" says Felicity.

"Granma, you're on fire!" says Chastity.

You'd think the whole place was on fire. The corridors flicker with excitement, everybody's rushing along past the "Do Not Obstruct" signs, all the sliding doors are opening by themselves as if they don't even need a whatsitsname. The Ragnarök girl rushes past me in one direction, the Götterdämmerung girl in another.

As I pass through the dining room, even the ones in their wheel-chairs lined up against the wall beneath the picture of the smiling sharks seem to be excited, or at least alive.

I move through it all like flame.

Nothing can stop me.

Then something stops me.

It is the Angry Nurse.

She stands there before me in the corridor.

She has a pillow.

She smiles.

I have come so close.

I have made things happen.

It has not been enough.

Now she will kill me.

"There you are, dear," she says.

She doesn't even try to hide the pillow.

"I was coming for you," she says.

"Of course you were," I say. "Here I am."

The Angry Nurse and I understand each other.

"I am not afraid," I tell her.

It's a lie. Things are happening, and I am afraid I will not see them happen.

That smile of hers. That pillow.

"I am not afraid," I say again, and I know she knows it isn't true.

"Of course you're not, my dear," she says.

She is very good at what she does.

"You can't stop it," I tell her.

That pillow.

"Stop it?" she says.

That smile.

"You can't stop it, whatever you do to me. I have changed my password. My son, and even my daughter, have blown whistles. And now all sorts of things are changing. And nothing you do can stop it."

"Stop it?" she says again. "Stop it?"

And then the strangest thing happens.

The Angry Nurse laughs.

"Oh dear," she says, still laughing. "I don't want to stop it. Dear me, no. The last thing I would want to do is stop it!"

"But," I tell her, "that pillow?"

"There's always someone who needs a pillow," she says.

"But, surely," I say. "You want to kill me, surely?"

"I don't want to kill anybody, dear," she says. "And don't call me Shirley."

She's still laughing.

"But aren't you angry?"

"Of course I'm angry," she says. "I'm the Angry Nurse!"

She's still laughing.

"My son . . ." I say.

"Your son is a very good boy," she says. "I couldn't have done it without him."

"You couldn't?"

"Or you, dear, of course. None of this would have happened without you."

"None? This? Me?"

"You have done something. Somehow you have done something that has long needed doing. I have wanted to do something, but what could I do? I've been waiting for this for so long. Now you have done something for all of us. And you have done something for your son and your daughter, by making *them* do something. And what you have all done has done so much for all of us. For all the poor souls here in this place. For . . . all of us."

"And now?"

"Now I can do something too. I have watched. I have listened. For a long time I have been collecting . . ."

"Not just pillows?"

"Evidence, my dear. And now . . ."

"And now? What will the Scare Manager do?"

"He will assist the police with their inquiries. He will not obstruct. It will be Best Practice, going forward."

I'm not sure she will ever stop laughing.

"Things never change," she says. "Until they do. Then they change very quickly."

And I see the head of my first husband atop his mighty neck. With one sudden stroke, it is gone.

"Very quickly indeed," I say.

And I see the nice boy writing *forget* in the big diary. And *forgive*.

"I am worried about the nice boy who mops the floors," I say.

"Don't worry, she will be okay," the Nurse tells me. "I will keep my eye on her. I have always kept my eye on her."

She sees my what do you call it. Astonishment.

"It's Holistic." She laughs.

I think of the nice boy's fringe and his breasts. Things don't change, until they do.

"Will I get my room back? My real, actual room? The one with trees in the window instead of a parking lot? Without any piece of silk tied to the door handle?"

"You can have it all, dear. You can have everything."

"I don't want it," I tell her. "I don't need it. I don't need anything."

I just keep on astonishing myself.

All I need is my son and my daughter. Who, whom, I did not love enough when they needed me most. And Felicity and Charity, who are the future, and have such smart thumbs. And the nice boy, with her mysterious bosom and her mop-like fringe and her earrings and her way of always being sideways.

The Hippocratic girl rushes past us with a cup of tea for someone.

"You have always . . . ?" I say to the Nurse.

"Always."

"You have never . . . ?"

"Not for a moment."

"Now I see it all," I tell her. "Now I understand everything." Which is not entirely true, but whatever.

"There's always more," she says.

"Nevertheless."

We understand each other, the Nurse and I.

"You're on fire, Rose!"

It doesn't even matter that it's not my name.

"It really is Person-Centered!" I say.

"Bingo!" says the Nurse.

She touches my shoulder. Gently. And laughs. Like a lunatic.

"Now, I need to get this pillow to someone who needs it. And you need to keep going. You don't want to miss anything."

And she leaves me. And I keep going. I am on fire.

I charge along the corridors, past various "Do Not Obstruct" signs, to the revelator. The doors are held open for me by two policemen, one of whom is a policewoman. They look like angels going up to heaven. But they aren't going up. They're going down, and they're taking the Scare Manager with them.

He stands there in the open revelator, between the two angels. He looks at me. No he doesn't. I don't know what he looks at, what he sees. I never have, really. I doubt if he has ever seen me or any other of the poor souls in this place. The only thing he has ever seen, perhaps, is his vision of all that beautiful gold.

The police invite me to join them in their . . . descent, but I decline the offer. I read to them, mostly from memory, what the sign says about not being allowed to enter the revelator if you happen to be on fire.

"People keep telling me I'm on fire," I explain.

The revelator doors begin to close. The arrow points down, down, down, and makes its little noise. The two policewomen, one of whom is a policeman, both of whom are angels, each hold an arm of the Scare Manager.

Now he looks at me.

He looks scared. As if there will be very little gold where he's going, and even more fire.

"You look like the Scared Manager," I tell him. "Ha-ha."

His turtle doesn't look so golden now.

I feel pity for him.

No I don't. As if.

"I used to be scared too," I say. "But then I forgot."

He says nothing. He doesn't seem to have any of his usual words. I'd quite like to hear him try his bedside manners on me one last time. But he can't seem to manage it.

"You'll manage," I tell him. "We all manage. Until we don't."

And the fiery doors close, and down he goes.

I push open the nearest "Do Not Obstruct" sign, and my walker and I make our way down the Fiery Escape stairs. Which isn't easy, the stairs being so steep and neck-breaky. But there's no escaping me, and I finally reach the ground floor without, as far as I can tell, breaking my neck.

I head toward the main entrance and the parking lot with all the cameras and microscopes.

As I pass the office, I see the Nurse already sitting there behind her desk, laughing. Perhaps it took me even longer to get here than I thought. Nevertheless, here I am, so I did get here.

Also in the office with the Nurse are various angels and policewomen. And my son, and my daughter. And the nice boy, and the fellow who doesn't live here. They all seem to be agreeing upon something.

Perhaps it is change which they are agreeing upon. Upon which they are agreeing. That change is good, perhaps. Or at least agreed upon.

The big sliding entrance doors open and close by themselves as if there is no longer any secret code or never was one.

The police come and go with their boxes and files and meatballs, and the two angels push their way out through the cameras
and microscopes, each holding an arm of the Scared Manager.
They move through the parking lot, past the golden motorbike
that has been left in the special space marked "Scared Manager,"
now all fenced around with bright-colored whatsitsname like a
crime on TV.

People point microscopes at the Scared Manager and ask him
questions, but he doesn't answer. He seems to have forgotten his
way with words, his bedside manners. He appears smaller, as
well as much less golden.

The angels move him toward a police car, ready and waiting
to take him somewhere nice. Or at least appropriate, going forward.

People talk with great seriousness and understanding into
their microscopes, while other people point cameras at them. At
this very moment they will be appearing, I imagine, on TVs
hanging high in corners everywhere, while others sit side by side
behind coffee cups and agree with each other.

My walker and I go out through the big doors and into the
crowd. I am not about to miss this.

I have made this happen.

Someone even sticks a microscope in my face and asks me a
question.

How do I feel, something like that.

But I don't have any answers.

"Zbtosmty," I say.

I know that right now, hanging from a ceiling somewhere,
I am on a TV being watched by someone with their mouth
open.

And here I am also, in this parking lot. My friend is here too.
She lies on her back, staring up at the sky. She wears her meatball-
stained nightgown. The blue whatsitsnames around her neck,
Myosotis scorpioides, forget-me-nots, are the same color as the sky.
And, I realize, her eyes.

The Scared Manager has almost reached the waiting police car.

And something wonderful is happening.

The parking lot is becoming a kind of garden.

Its concrete appears to flow, to flower.

Its straight lines and rectangles go wild, its edges are uncontained.

As well as *Myosotis scorpioides*, there is *Lactuca sativa* and *Corymbia maculata* and *Acacia baileyana* and *Brunfelsia grandiflora*. Yesterday-today-tomorrow. And roses, of course. Rows and rose of Roses.

And there in a corner of this garden parking lot, surrounded by leaves and flowers and sunshine, is a bench. An older fellow sits on this bench, holding hands with a woman. Even from this distance I can see what a beautiful neck he has. He squeezes the woman's hand, she squeezes back, as if neither of them will ever let go. Nevertheless. I don't know her name.

One of the angels opens the rear door of the police car, introducing the Scared Manager to the back seat as if he may never have seen such a thing before.

I don't need to watch. I know what will happen.

They help him inside and then drive him slowly away, being very, very careful with his head.

I am more interested in something else. A sound.

No, a noise.

It is loud, and getting louder, so loud it must be what do you call it, magnified, by all the microscopes.

And it is bright, like sunshine and forget-me-nots and the rainbow flash of a lunatic's wings.

Trichoglossus moluccanus.

Screeching, squealing, squawking, screaming in the light.

They fly right through the parking lot, first one and then another and another and then others, a magnificent flock of rainbow lunatics. And a cockatoo or two. They fly right at me, through me, instead of me, flying right where my head should be.

All I can do is laugh.

Which is what I do in that bright, noisy parking lot until the nice boy comes out to join me. She puts her arm around me and we begin to move away together, backward and sideways and in other directions that are entirely our own, so that all the people wanting answers are left there with their cameras and microscopes, and a sky filled with lunatics.

Things never change, until they do. Nothing ever happens, then things happen very quickly. It's about time.

Everything about this place is different, even if it isn't.

Everyone seems happier, about their room at least, or about the wall that they sit against in their wheelchair, or whatever.

None of us may have much more in our accounts, but what we have at least flows in a new direction.

One day recently there was a quiz night, and someone got an answer right.

There is even some talk of the meatballs having improved.

The poor souls in their wheelchairs still sit against the wall beneath the picture of the smiling sharks, but you sometimes see them with big grins on their faces as they take turns wearing a golden motorcycle helmet.

And now here we all are together in my room. There is a piece of silk on the door handle that tells me it's my room, anyway, and why would I argue? The TV high up in the corner shows people driving cars too fast through rivers, as if they are in a great hurry to get somewhere nice, or else eating hamburgers with one hand while they dance and sing, or sitting at a desk behind coffee cups agreeing with each other. Out the window there is a garden, or a parking lot, I really don't care which. Because there is an older fellow out there with me, and we hold hands in the sunshine and there are trees and flowers and the noise of birds. And whether there are trees and flowers and birds out that window or whether there are not, it appears that I know their names. *Maculata*. Crepuscule. *Lactuca*. *Trichoglossus moluccanus*. *Callocephalon fimbriatum*. These are words that I know. The older fellow and I both know them, together. And they are not all the words we know. Sometimes we even say the words to each other.

I love you.

And I love you.

And here in my room, here we all are. My son and my daughter are here, together, which is strange, although not unpleasant. And what is possibly even stranger, and even pleasanter, is that I am washing both their toes. I am washing the toes of both of them. My son and my daughter. This embarrasses them, of course, but that isn't the only reason I do it. It is to show them, to let them know. Even without the words. Any moment now I might even tickle these toes of theirs, and they might perhaps even giggle and look up at me with love, although of course I do not wish to push my luck.

My dear son has even brought his wife along to visit. It is delightful to have her here, particularly since she so clearly wishes she were somewhere else. I expect her at any moment to call me an impossible old cow. I am doing my best.

I have moved the photo of my headless first husband, in its nice new frame, right to the edge of the whatsitsname, in front of the rest of the smiling Dresser family. My children enjoy seeing it there, which doesn't even annoy me.

At the window, with their backs turned to the garden, or parking lot, are Felicity and Charity with their thumbs and their smart phones, which is strange, since they are away at university and at least one of them is having trouble with biology.

The Nurse is laughing and hitting my knee with a tiny hammer. She has brought me an extra pillow and a Scrabble board. When she finishes with that hammer, we will have a lovely time playing Scrabble together. She is quite good at it, although I am still trying to teach her how to cheat.

The Crepuscular girl brings tea. A girl brings tea, anyway. I have no idea what she is, where she comes from. Perhaps I will try to find out.

The nice boy is in my bathroom, which is trans-friendly. He is doing something sideways with his bosom. I'm not sure if God, or Jesus or whatever, is involved, and it's none of my business anyway. The boy needs her privacy.

And here too is the fellow who doesn't live here. I can see by the look on his face that he wants to explain everything to me. Silly old bugger. I am very fond of him. Just for old times' sake, I ask him what floor he is on.

"Oh," he says, looking astonished, "I don't live here!"

"I can't tell you," I reply, "how happy it makes me to hear you say that."

"Mom," says my daughter, "you're tickling me!" And she giggles with delight. Well, perhaps not, but nevertheless.

Oh, and there is a Chihuahua here somewhere. Where is a penguin when you need one?

The big diary lies open on the whatsitsname. I don't need to look at it. I know what's in there. I know what will happen.

I don't care what's out that window, really, and I don't care about my password. My son and my daughter both have my password and as far as I can tell it makes them happy, or something. And of course they both have the Power of Eternal. My son appears to be getting over his hiccups, and if his bottom will never be quite as clean as it once was, well, whatever. And now my daughter has a whole new set of things to be busy and tired about, since Electricity and Chutney went off to university and the nice boy took over my bathroom.

As for me, I don't need a password. I don't even need a name. I remind myself sometimes of how that lunatic in the garden flew, laughing like a lorikeet, right where my head was, or once had been. Not being careful with it at all. People are too careful, perhaps, with people's heads. Nevertheless. Nothing can stop the remembering and the forgetting and the understanding and the misunderstanding and the loving and the losing, until something does.

In the meantime, and even in the mean times, this is enough. I have become Rose. It is as good a name as any. Perhaps Rose is my password, perhaps I am hers.

I know what I know.

I am what I am.

Anything else is what do you call it.

Zbtosmty.

ACKNOWLEDGMENTS

To all at Atria, and at Allen & Unwin Australia, your enthusiasm and care and professionalism in the service of this book is a dream come true for its author.

Massive thanks to my agent, Melanie Ostell, who "got" Rose from the start, then pushed me to make the book all that it could be. Your clear eye and straight talk are much appreciated.

Thanks to international rights agents Nerrilee Weir and Fiona Henderson of Bold Type for taking Rose around the world.

Thanks to my mom, Ollie, for the cheerful indomitability. And thanks to my mother-in-law, Joy, for the inappropriateness and the penguins.

And to Deborah. All the words I know could never be enough.

ABOUT THE AUTHOR

B ruce Nash is the author of two previous novels, *An Island in the Lake* (2019) and *The Long River of Cat Fisher* (2020). He lives on the far south coast of New South Wales, where he writes and makes habitat on Djiringanj Country, by the shores of Wallaga Lake.